BRUTAL MOON

Andrew Morris
Laura Dodd

A TIME & FATE ADVENTURE GAMEBOOK

by

ANDREW MORRIS & LAURA DODD

TIME and FATE
.com

Brutal Moon
Copyright © 2023 Andrew Morris and Laura Dodd
First Published: May 2023
Publisher: TimeandFate.com
ISBN: 9798391114765
Fiction
Paperback First Edition

The right of Andrew Morris and Laura Dodd to be identified as the authors of this work has been asserted by them in accordance with sections 77 and 78 of the Copyright, Designs and Patents Act 1988.

All rights reserved. No part of this publication may be reproduced, stored in retrieval system, copied in any form or by any means, electronic, mechanical, photocopying, recording or otherwise transmitted without written permission from the author(s) except for the use of brief quotations in literary reviews. You must not circulate this book in any format.

This is a work of fiction. Names, characters, businesses, organisations, places, events, locales, and incidents are either the products of the authors' imaginations or used in a fictitious manner. Any resemblance to actual persons, living or dead, or actual events is purely coincidental.

Book cover and internal illustrations by Andrew Morris.

Contents

How to Play	007
Essentially, Hilary Hills	008
You are in SItU	009
Things You Should Know	012
Brutal Moon	015
Acknowledgements	239
Closing Credits	242
Hilary's Notepad	243

```
INCOMING COMMS FROM:
LEIUTENANT CLAIRE LAWSON

MAYDAY + + + MAYDAY + + +

MOONBASE SHACKLETON UNDER ATTACK + + +
SATURMEKS HAVE INVADED + + +
CREW DEAD + + +
COMMANDER MISSING PRESUMED LOST + + +
SATURMEKS PLAN TO - - -
          [TRANSMISSION INTERRUPTED]
SEND HELP. THEY MUST BE STOPPED!
         - - - - - - - - - - - [SIGNAL LOST]
```

How to Play
BRUTAL MOON

In *Brutal Moon* you play the part of Hilary Hills, a member of the *Department of Scientific Investigation into the Uncanny* (SItU), who has been assigned to act as assistant to their Chief Scientist, a profoundly intelligent and enigmatic woman named Professor Vyvian Wylie. What begins as a pretty routine day quickly becomes a life-or-death situation as you find yourself stranded alone on a Moonbase one hundred years into the future.

Brutal Moon is an example of branching literature, and follows the well-established format of the Adventure Gamebooks which became immensely popular in the late 1970s and throughout the 1980s. Playing the game is simple; read the story introduction at *Reference 001* and follow the instructions from there. Throughout the story you will be regularly offered choices of what you should do next, with each option instructing you to turn to a specific reference as you make your way along one of the many diverging and converging paths the story can take. Each decision made will have outcomes and consequences which can lead to either your success or failure.

There's no fighting in this fantasy, nor are there any moments when only pure luck will see you through, so dice-rolling and coin-flipping are not necessary during this particular adventure.

A pencil, though, even a nibbled 2B one, might prove quite handy.

Essential extracts from the personnel file of
HILARY KEMPSEY HILLS.
Confidential.

Born 1950.
Cambridge Graduate 1971.
Masters Degree 1973.
Currently studying for PHD.

Awarded internship with Top-Secret Ministry of Defence Department of Scientific Investigation into the Uncanny (SItU) at behest of Great Uncle, Sir Melvern Hills OBE.

Hilary Hills reports directly to SItU Scientific Head, Professor Vyvian Wylie. Wylie commented on recent assessment documents that she finds Hills to be...

Pro; Resourceful, Demonstrates courage in face of Adversity, Keen to take initiative, Empathic, Abstract thinker, Highly intelligent.

Con; Displays bohemian tendencies, Bit of a day-dreamer, Easily bored, Occasionally questions or challenges authority.

You are in SItU

"It was an uncommonly tempestuous storm that thundered across the country the night that the unearthly invaders struck at Britain. The metal creatures, thought to have hailed from Mars, and who resembled self-propelled pillar boxes, made no attempt to announce themselves or state their intentions, but instead immediately and brutally set to bringing about the decimation and subjugation of mankind."

Erwin S. Ramrod,
Society Diarist, Dec. 1897.

"Although the Empire had been ever vigilant against the machinations of foreign powers, we had never considered the possibility of an attack from another world. The peculiar atmospheric conditions, strange lights in the sky, and sightings of goblins in rural areas during the week preceding the attack should have put us on our guard, but we failed to see the significance of these portents. Henceforth, I suggest that such phenomena be viewed with great suspicion, and diligently assessed to determine if a threat is presented. Gentlemen, there is a definite and immediate need to establish a body of experts to scientifically investigate any and all such uncanny events."

Sir Matthew White Ridley,
Secretary of State for the Home Department
from the Minutes of a Cabinet Meeting, Feb. 1898.

"...I have therefore established a Department of Scientific Investigation into the Uncanny; an unprecedented assembly of our finest scientists, engineers, and thinkers. Although this will be predominantly a civilian body, it will operate under the auspices of the War Office. Sir George Darwin has been appointed the Department's Scientific Lead, and the group will be overseen by Henry Petty-Fitzmaurice, your Secretary of State for War."

> Prime Minister Robert Gascoyne-Cecil,
> in a letter to Her Royal Highness Queen Victoria
> March, 1898.

"We approve of your initiative, but must insist that the existence of such a group be kept from the public for the sake of national morale. The people must be protected from the knowledge that many similar counter-natural threats loom over our World."

> Queen Victoria, replying to Gascoyne-Cecil.
> March, 1898.

"Interviewed 'Prof. Q.' for Science Lead position with SItU, now that Hoyle's stepped down. Heard that he's a loose cannon, and found him to be an opinionated curmudgeon. Unsuitable. By chance, however, was also introduced to his deputy, Prof. Vyvian Wylie. Offered her the job within five minutes of meeting her. Serendipity!"

> Sir Clive Browne, MP,
> Secretary of State for Defence.
> Extract from his personal diary, July 16th 1969.

"Hilary. Managed to land you a plum role. A science thing for the Government. Rather hush-hush. Internship. Pay not great but, by golly, this is a major rung on the ladder for you. Meet me at my Whitehall residence Monday morning, 8ish, and I'll introduce you to my old bat-man, Sir Clive.
      – Uncle Mel."

Sir Melvern Hills, OBE.
A hand-written letter, Wed. 29th Aug., 1973.

"Mott the Hoople's new LP is out today! Will try and pick it up when I'm in London on Monday. Got to visit Uncle Melvern then – he reckons he's got me a job."

Hilary Hills.
Personal diary entry, Fri. 31st Aug., 1973.

Things You Should Know

Make a few notes as you go.
You're likely to find essential information during your adventure, and to ensure you don't overlook it the story text will prompt you to *make a careful note of* it. You'll find a page from Hilary Hills' notepad at the rear of this book on which you can jot a few things down. Take a quick look now; you'll see that there's already a note of what's stuffed in Hilary's back pocket this morning.

Mental? Map!
Mental maps are good if you have a keen sense of direction, but pencil-and-paper maps are probably better when you're Hilary Hills and you find yourself in a crazy situation like this! The Moonbase isn't huge, but there are a few sharp turns and dead ends, so scribbling a little lay-out of the Moonbase as you go might be beneficial.

Prose.
Cardinal directions and certain nouns in this story will be described and referred to using Capital Letters even when not grammatically necessary. It's a naming convention used in some gamebooks which not only helps the player maintain their bearings but also makes potentially useful inventory items more immediately recognisable.

Savvy Scoring.
Hilary, being a University Student in the 1970s, is pretty hip an' mod, so you'll have to forgive the unconventional term Hills uses to refer to intelligence gathered during the adventure. You'll find that you'll be awarded points to add to your *Savvy Score* throughout the story, record these points accurately because you'll need to tally them up at the end of the game.

But Don't Get Too Savvy!

Please note; you can only take Savvy Points *once* from any location, so if you find yourself visiting a location for a second time and being offered a second helping of Savvy for repeating an action you've done before, you shouldn't take them. Doing so would only spoil the ending for you!

You *Are* Hilary Hills.

If you haven't already, you'll benefit from reading the extracts from Hilary's personnel file back on page eight. Be true to your character and act accordingly. You're up against time, and Hilary Hills' fate is in your hands.
Good luck!

001

Sir Clive Browne had cautioned you, and in retrospect you think he was only half-joking, that most of your time as Professor Vyvian Wylie's assistant would be spent passing her tools and reminding her how brilliant she was. That was a little over six months ago, and although it's fair to say that you do actually spend some of your time taking care of the Professor's laboratory equipment, or soothing her occasionally fractured pride, a majority of your work in the service of SItU's Scientific Head has been eventful to say the least.

You had been forewarned that the Professor was, well, special. She's eccentric, gregarious, jaunty and garrulous, with a bent for adventure and a nose for trouble. In the past few weeks alone, she's taken you out into the field on several occasions to scientifically investigate and appraise unexplained, and sometimes inexplicable, occurrences that might pose a threat to Britain's security. There were sightings of ape-like hominids near caves in Devon, a fishing boat attacked by something large, dark and scaly off Scarborough's coast, and, oh... the less said about the large glob of green slime that oozed up from the Clootie Well in Culloden and ate a walker's dog the better!

So, although it's fair to say that you graduated from being the Professor's toolbox monkey a while ago, there are still days, like today, when matters are no more pressing than to watch Professor Wylie tinker on her various top-secret projects whilst you occasionally ask a pertinent question to remind her how brilliant she is.

Professor Wylie is currently stood at her workbench, which is situated right in the middle of her spacious laboratory, and is thoroughly engrossed in examining and dismantling a battered and scorched rectangular metal box about the size and shape of a domestic refrigerator. She had two burly squaddies lug the thing in yesterday morning and, judging by the numerous drained coffee cups and half-eaten sandwiches that litter her workspace, you suspect that the Professor's been tinkering with this metal refrigerator or *whatever-it-is* ever since. You notice she looks tired; dark rings are appearing around her usually bright eyes, and her silvery-blond hair is rather carelessly tied back in an untidy bun.

You're perched on a stool at your own modest workbench, soldering copper-core wires to a somewhat jury-rigged circuit board, diligently following a pencil-scrawl-on-napkin schematic so typical of the Professor. The circuit, she'd explained earlier, whilst jabbing at her doodle with her nibbled 2B pencil, was a speculative idea, *a mere whimsy,* she'd said, but might be the key to unlocking the mysteries of her latest investigation.

Despite her obvious tiredness, and keen focus on the metal case, Professor Wylie's been chatting the entire morning as she's worked; regaling you with stories of her year spent working covertly behind the Iron Curtain, and of her subsequent stint with the *Britannic Experimental Rocket Group*, initially as a test pilot and later as deputy to a chap she refers to fondly – as if you know who she's talking about – as Bernie.

"If my suspicions about this piece of crash wreckage are correct and we get it working again, we'll have to invite Bernie over to watch a demonstration, Hills," suggests the Professor as she fishes the vital-looking fist-sized sphere from deep within the body of the case. She studies the component with an expression of mercurial delight; it has six one-inch-long tubular limbs protruding from it, and at the end of each limb is a matchbox-sized unit.

"Er... what exactly are your suspicions, Professor," you reply, keeping your eyes focused on a particularly tricky bit of soldering. You've finished fixing the wires in place and are now attaching terminals to the battery housing.

"Oh, I've not told you, have I? Hmm, need to know basis, Hills," replies the Professor as she unscrews one of the matchbox sized things from the end of its tube.

"Hmmph," you mumble despondently. You hate it when the Professor keeps you in the dark.

Professor Wylie looks up from her work and observes you momentarily with her hands on her hips and a look of exaggerated astonishment on her face.

"Hurrumph?!" she gasps in mock surprise. "Well, since you put forward such a convincing case for elucidation..." then she gives you a gentle smile.

"You know about the UFO that crashed in Wales? The Berwyn Mountains area?"

"A couple of months ago, yeah," you reply. "Witnesses say they heard a loud noise and saw a bright light in the sky. Then the area was hit by a bit of an earthquake."

"The official story is, of course, that the light in the sky was a meteor, and the minor earthquake was coincidence. Given a bit more time we might've come up with a more convincing lie, but the Press was haranguing the MOD for answers."

"So, this case you're taking apart is debris from a crashed alien craft?" you ask as you take a *C-size Eveready* and slot it into place on the circuit to test your soldering work. You note with quiet satisfaction that the small bulb in the circuit illuminates; this Wylie-designed, napkin-scrawled thingamajig is working!

"Not exactly," replies the Professor airily, now prodding a screwdriver down the hollow arm and into the heart of the fist-sized component. "I think it was a time machine from the future which broke apart and exploded in mid-air as it arrived in our time."

You chuckle, thinking the Professor must be in a knavish mood.

"No, I'm serious," she continues. "Most of the craft was atomised... er, as was the pilot, presumably. We recovered what we could, including this heavy chunk of technology. Some of the components inside this housing, which I think, by the way, might be the craft's time-engine, are stamped with manufacturer's marks and serial numbers written in plain English. This part, for instance, has a little boiler-plate riveted to it that reads 'Tachyon Capacitor Mark Two-Point-Five'."

Professor Wylie pauses for a moment, as if considering her next words carefully.

"Should I tell Hills?" she mutters, as she briefly slips into her peculiar habit of having a conversation with herself. "No. Yes. No, better not. Ah! Yes, what the heck!"

Professor Wylie slips her hand back into the crash debris casing, takes a firm grasp on something out of your sight, gives it a twist, and then a tug, and you hear the clunk of an engine component disengage. She withdraws her hand, brandishing a whitish-grey cylinder, probably made from a ceramic material, the size and shape of a roll of toilet paper.

"Look at this, Hills," she says, with more than a hint of exhilaration in her voice, as she crosses the lab towards you. "Look at what the maker's inscription on this engine part says!"

"The Vyvian Wylie Temporal Condenser Unit?!" you blurt, quoting the stamped text *ad verbatim*.

"Interesting, isn't it?" Professor Wylie replies with an enigmatic smile as she taps the cylinder with her finger. "It seems that at some point in the future I might invent a time-travel engine. As a matter of fact, the circuit you've been working on this morning is based on what's in here."

Your mind reels at the ramifications of the Professor's speculation as you gaze down at the jury-rigged circuit you've made. "But if you get this *Berwyn Device* repaired and operational again then, technically, you haven't really invented time travel. You've just... er..."

"Plagiarised the work of my future self!" exclaims the Professor, finishing your sentence as she returns to her own work bench, picks up the Tachyon Capacitor and resumes poking it with her screwdriver. "But where did the future Vyvian Wylie get her idea from? From what the present-day Vyvian Wylie discovered this morning? Oh, what a fascinating paradox! Y'know, I'm getting quite giddy just thinking ab... Argh! Ouch!"

The Professor's chit-chat is cut abruptly short by a sharp yelp of pain, and you immediately snap your head up to see what's caused her alarm. The rest happens so quickly; you see Professor Wylie recoiling, as if she's just received an electric shock, her arms thrown wide. Her mysterious Tachyon Capacitor tumbles to the floor, bounces twice and rolls to a stop. There's a brilliant flash, and suddenly a lightening bolt of blue-green energy arcs from within the

001

dropped device and repeatedly strikes at the ceiling. Then, like a riled cobra, the thin column of jagged light begins to strike out randomly to all corners of the room.

"Hilary," shouts the Professor over the ethereal crackle of raw, angry energy. "I think it's attracted to the circuit you're holding! Drop it and move!"

Too late, by a fraction of a second, just too late.

The energy arc stabs at the circuit board just at the very moment you loosen your grip and begin to slip from your stool...

...and then you're tumbling, falling...

...upwards, somehow.

There's no pain, no indignity of landing on the lab floor on your backside, no sound, even. There's just a tunnel of curling, dancing blue-green light along which you tumble toward a white void.

"Have I just died?" you wonder.

Then you hear the Professor's frantic voice, distinct and determined, echoing along the length of this whirlpool of luminance.

"Hills! Wherever you end up, stay put! Don't wander off! I'll get you back! I'll get you back... somehow!"

"Not dead, then," you whisper breathlessly to yourself, as Professor Wylie's echoing promise becomes increasingly distant before fading to silence.

Now turn to **024.**

002

You're disappointed to see that the shelves in the cabinet are almost entirely bare, the only exception being the middlemost shelf, which holds a square polystyrene tray. Within the tray are rounded indentations; four of the six indentations are empty, but the remaining two have hemispherical objects, that resemble cricket balls cut in half, nestling within them. It's sort of like an egg-box, if it's like anything you've seen before. You pick one of the hemispheres up and study the strange item; red, tough plastic with a gritty textured finish, seemingly solid, its flat side is covered with what appears to the glossy backing paper of adhesive tape.

Turn to **053**.

003

"Wha..?" you begin, blearily.

"The security console in the Operations Centre alerted us the instant you opened the Airlock to access the Lunar surface," states the Saturmek Drone. "We concluded that your intention was to activate the Moonbase Sterilisation Protocol. A futile gesture; we were aware that such a protocol was in place, and had over-ridden it using our superior Saturmek systems."

"But I was a goner. Why did you save my life?" you have to ask.

"Your physiognomy does not match with any of the eight crew members on record," states the Scientist Saturmek.

003

"And I have already eliminated all eight crew members," adds the Drone, in an almost boastful tone.

The Scientist scuttles closer to you, its electronic eye swivelling in its socket, surveying you up-and-down. You then watch, with some alarm, as the blue domed head of the Saturmek begins to slowly open with a pneumatic hiss, the front half swinging upward on a hinge like the visor of a motorcycle helmet, to reveal something within that you find truly alien and thoroughly unnerving; a single large eyeball, as big as your head, which appears to be neither mechanical nor actually organic, but an indefinable fusion of both. The eyeball has three pupils – one red, another green and the third blue – arranged triangularly, each glowing with an eerie internal energy. This grotesque and glistening orb protrudes from an oval, coppery socket that has fine grilles set into it, either side of the eyeball, which look rather like *hi-fi* speakers. Instinctively, and involuntarily, you take a step backward from the abhorrent sight.

"Remain still!" barks the Scientist, its voice no longer an electronic trill but a mucousy, guttural rasp. Its singular eye abruptly lurches forward, emerging from its armoured dome on the end of a ribbed fleshy tentacle, looking for all the word like an earthworm but as thick as your wrist. The flexible limb slithers out from the Saturmek casing and guides the eyeball closer to you, now taking on the alarming semblance of a serpent honing in on its prey. The eye studies you head-to-toe, its glowing pupils now pulsing in sequence as it pokes and nuzzles at parts of your trembling body like a police dog seeking contraband. You catch a whiff of the fetid odour that wafts from the fleshy tendril and try not to gag.

"My sensors detect vestigial traces of Chronon Radiation emanating from you," the Scientist states after what feels like a nauseating eternity.

"Theory; this is a time traveller," the Drone speculates.

"An anomaly," hisses the Scientist, as its eyeball slickly retreats back into its housing and then seals itself once more within its armoured blue dome. "An unanticipated variable!"

You get the impression that you've managed to cause the Saturmeks great inconvenience and annoyance simply by being here; you're a random and erratic element that they hadn't factored into their plan.

"We are going to hold you in detention," explains the Scientist. "And later, once we have returned to Titan, you will undergo a thorough examination and interrogation. If you have travelled through time to be here, we will want to know your secrets."

The Drone swivels its head-dome slowly to-and-fro, its illuminated eye-lens pulsing brightly, as if looking for something.

"Where should I detain the human?" it finally asks.

"Seal our prisoner in the South Airlock." commands the Scientist before turning to address you directly. "You will cause us no further trouble there. We will ensure you cannot escape. If you do attempt to resist or flee, we will have to reluctantly forfeit any scientific curiosity we have about your origins in favour of just killing you."

The Blue Saturmek's claw-like legs retract into its torso as it lowers itself onto its motivator ball. "Rejoin us in the Operations Centre once you have secured the prisoner," it orders the Drone. "We must use our combined processing abilities to complete our mission. This task takes priority over all other concerns."

The Scientist then exits at speed via the Red Airlock, and you watch it take a right turn at the end of the corridor.

Now turn to **042.**

004

There are four lockers standing in a row against the wall, and they are the tall, narrow metal type you often see in American High School movies. Each locker is identical to the next; they bear no name plates, nor any registration numbers or labels, in fact there's no personalisation at all. Each, you note with a wry smile, is locked by a simple combination tumbler; you reckon they should child's play to crack! But, of course, you realise, the lockers might be alarmed in some way against unauthorised access.

Do you want to risk opening one?

If you want to crack the combination of one of the lockers, turn to **139.**

If you feel you'd best leave the lockers well alone, just in case, then turn to **111.**

005

You're suddenly wracked with utter horror as you realise your elementary mistake! Your vision becomes milky as your eyes fall upon the laminated notice on the door:

Spacesuits must be worn by all personnel present in chamber during ingress or egress of work party.

The temperature in the chamber falls rapidly, and it quickly becomes impossible to breath; the very air is being sucked from your lungs!

"I don't want to die!" you think through the fog of fear. "This is a horrible way to go!"

Your knees buckle, and you crumple to the floor. Your last thoughts are of Professor Wylie; you're afraid she'll suffer a similar, grisly fate when she finally manages to reach Moonbase Shackleton meaning to rescue you.

Then all is darkness and silence as you, Hilary Hills, out of place and out of time, die on the Moon in the year 2074AD.

The End.

006

Swiftly, silently and with great circumspect, you creep down the lengthy East Corridor towards the sturdy Red Airlock Door.

Looking even heftier than the previous doorways you've passed through; this portal reminds you of those bank vault doors you're seen in old heist movies. There must be something really important behind here.

Once you've spun the locking wheel a few twists anti-clockwise, and despite its size and obvious weight, the windowless, unmarked door swings silently open with hydraulically-assisted ease.

Wary that you might be heading into mortal danger, you step through into the room beyond.

Now turn to **161**.

007

Making yourself as small and unobtrusive as humanly possible, you crouch behind the bank of terminals and peer through a narrow gap between two units. You're quietly delighted to find that you can both clearly see and hear the Saturmeks and all that transpires between them.

"Shackleton Research Records show that the Moonbase scientists hypothesised the symbols and patterns upon this artefact were a hieroglyphic cipher to unlocking the secrets of this satellite's propulsion units."

"They thought it contained instructions?"

"They were foolish to pursue this line of reasoning. The etchings on the faces of this obelisk are meaningless. There is no code here to decipher."

"The symbols are purely decorative. The makers of this artefact embellished it with etchings that they found aesthetically pleasing."

"Deep Röntgen Analysis shows that there's a complex crystalline matrix at the core of this object. Conclusion; this artefact is part of a circuit."

"Its function is that of a circuit-breaker or fuse."

"Or a capacitor."

"We must locate where within the Moon's interior this item was discovered. Reinstatement to its correct location should restore this satellite's propulsion units to full working order."

"We can then ignite the Lunar engines and plunge this Moon into Earth's atmosphere. The collision between Earth and its satellite will cause the planet to fracture."

"We will bring about the total annihilation of all life on Earth!"

"We will wreak our absolute revenge. We will destroy that which we cannot possess!"

The sheer scale and downright monstrousness of the Saturmek plan is enough to send a chill up your spine, and what's even more horrifying is that they're so close to achieving their aim. You must do something to prevent this atrocity!

Now add 20 points to your Savvy Score and turn to **050.**

008

"You are an enemy of the Saturmeks," it gloats as it closes in. "You must die!"

A hatch in the side of the Saturmek's barrel-like body opens and out snakes a long, flexible arm at the end of which is a vicious-looking circular saw. You note with horror that the ragged teeth of the glistening disk are clogged with dried blood and tatters of flesh. The blade whirrs into life, becoming a spinning ruddy blur, with a mechanical whine which all-too-much resembles that of a dentist's drill, as the robotic sadist advances towards you.

You shut your eyes, hoping it will all be over quickly.

"Wait!" you hear a second Saturmek voice, and it carries a deeper and more commanding tone.

Cautiously opening one eye, you watch as your would-be executioner slowly turns to face its Red Commander, which is now rolling up the corridor to join you.

"The physiognomy of this human does not match with any of the eight crew members on record," states the Red Saturmek.

"I have already killed the entire crew," adds the Drone, in an almost boastful tone.

The Commander scuttles closer to you, its electronic eye swivelling in its socket, surveying you up-and-down. You then watch, with some alarm, as the red domed head of the Saturmek begins to slowly open with a pneumatic hiss, the front half swinging upward on a hinge like the visor of a motorcycle helmet, to reveal something within that you find truly alien and thoroughly unnerving; a single large eyeball, as big as your head, which appears to be neither fully mechanical nor actually organic, but an

indefinable fusion of both. The eyeball has three pupils – one red, another green and the third blue – arranged triangularly, each glowing with an eerie internal energy. This grotesque and glistening orb protrudes from an oval, coppery socket that has fine grilles set into it, either side of the eye, which somewhat resemble *hi-fi* speakers. Instinctively, and involuntarily, you take a single, hasty step backward from the abhorrent sight.

"Remain still!" barks the Saturmek Commander, its voice no longer an electronic trill but a mucousy, guttural rasp. Its singular eye abruptly lurches forward, emerging from its armoured dome on the end of a ribbed fleshy tentacle, looking for all the word like an earthworm but as thick as your wrist. The flexible limb slithers out from the Saturmek casing and guides the eyeball closer to you, now taking on the alarming semblance of a serpent honing in on its prey. The eye studies you up-and-down, its glowing pupils now pulsing in sequence as it pokes and nuzzles at parts of your trembling body like a police dog seeking contraband. You catch a whiff of the fetid odour that wafts from the fleshy tendril and try not to gag.

"My sensors detect vestigial traces of Chronon Radiation emanating from you," the Commander states after what seems like a nauseating eternity.

"Theory; you are a time traveller," the Drone speculates.

"An anomaly!" growls the Commander, as its eyeball slickly retreats back into its housing and then seals itself once more within its armoured dome. "An unanticipated variable!"

You get the impression that you've managed to cause the Saturmeks great inconvenience and annoyance simply by being here; you're a random and erratic element that they hadn't factored into their plan.

"You are to be held in detention," orders the Commander. "Later, once we have return to Titan, you will be subjected to a thorough examination and interrogation. If you have travelled through time to be here, we will want to know your secrets."

The Drone swivels its head-dome slowly to-and-fro, its illuminated eye-lens pulsing brightly, as if looking for something.

"Where should I detain the human, Leader?" it finally asks.

"Seal our prisoner in the South Airlock." commands the Red Saturmek before turning to address you directly. "You will cause us no further trouble there. We will ensure you cannot escape. And if you do attempt to resist or flee, we will gladly forfeit any scientific curiosity we have about your origins in favour of just killing you."

The Red Saturmek's claw-like legs retract into its torso as it lowers itself onto its motivator ball. "Join me and the others in the Operations Centre once you have secured the prisoner," it orders the Drone. "We must combine our processing abilities to continue to decrypt the Shackleton Artefact. This task takes priority over all other concerns."

The Red Chief Saturmek then glides Northward up the Main Corridor towards the Green Internal Airlock.

Add 10 points to your Savvy Score.

There's still a decent few yards separating you from the blood-spattered Saturmek. Here's your chance to make a break for it down the East Corridor if you think you should.

Do you chance a mad dash for it? If so, turn to **081**.

Or do you continue to co-operate and allow yourself to be imprisoned awaiting examination and interrogation? To play it safe, turn to **042**.

009

You draw a sharp breath through gritted teeth, hoping to correctly recall the late Commander's Authorisation Code. Asterisks appear on-screen as you tap the numerical keys, and with the last digit typed in, you step back expectantly.

Nothing happens.

You wait a few moments more before studying the screen again. Your asterisks remain on the display beneath the phrase:

ENTER LOGIN.

"Enter?" you mutter, baffled by this futuristic keyboard.

You then notice a key on the right-hand side of the keypad which contains a diagram of a downward arrow bending back on itself, rather like the return key on your electric typewriter at SItU HQ. You draw a second deep breath, chose to trust your intuition, and press it.

The screen goes blank momentarily before fresh text is displayed:

LOGIN AUTHORISED.

THANK YOU, COMMANDER KING.

"Groovy!" you exclaim.

Now turn to **025**.

010

You've heard more than enough to know that Earth is in the most terrible, imminent peril! But what can you do? You need a few moments to think... preferably somewhere safer than here!

You notice what looks to be a miniaturised walkie-talkie in a recharger dock atop the terminal behind which you hide, and you dare a moment to snatch and pocket it. Perhaps, once you're clear of this area you can radio an alert to Earth.

As you continue observation, the Saturmeks become more animated, gesturing with their metal limbs and swivelling their domes. You know you must stay cool, be patient, and watch keenly for an opportunity to sneak out unseen.

The Green Drones discuss moving the Obelisk Artefact to the Shackleton Well, but the Scientist interrupts with news that it has detected both the Well and the Moonbase itself are mined with atomic explosives as part of a self-destruct procedure called Sterilisation Protocol Alpha One. Their Commander comments that it was fortuitous their attack was so swift and merciless that the Moonbase crew had no time to activate it.

There is a parallel Self-Destruct Control Terminal situated in the Administrator's Cabin near the Well itself, but the Scientist is certain that deactivating Sterilisation Protocol Alpha One here in the Operations Centre will also nullify the terminal outside. The Commander agrees that before entering the Moon's interior it would be prudent to hack and deactivate the Self-Destruct System. The system is password protected, so this will take some little time.

Now turn to **083.**

011

You enter the Airlock and meekly settle cross-legged on the floor. The Saturmek studies you for a moment and, once satisfied that you'll cause no further trouble, it casts its electronic eye about the small chamber. It pauses for a moment to study the eight Spacesuits hanging on the wall, then it levels its chest-gun towards them and fires a low-intensity beam. You watch with carefully-masked dismay as the suits char and crumble to dust. You were hoping to use one of those to make an escape to outside, but the Saturmek clearly anticipated your scheme.

The Airlock Door slams shut, and you rise to your feet to watch through the port-hole as the Green Saturmek glides up the corridor to join its cohort.

"Hurry, Professor," you mutter as you turn your back on the door. "I really don't like the sound of being examined and interrogated."

Now turn to **052**.

012

"Help's coming," you say, placing your faith in Professor Wylie. "Estimated just thirty minutes away. You're not going to die."

"I'm already dead," Lawson's cough is almost a chuckle. "I'm a cyborg; forty-two percent machine. My human side's as good as dead already. It's my cybernetics that are keeping me going, but they're failing too... trying to repair me, but can't. I'm far too damaged."

"But Professor Wylie..." you start, grasping Lawson's hand and finding it deathly cold.

"Need a wily mechanic, not a Wylie Professor," interrupts Lawson with a hint of sardonic humour.

You need to know what you should do, and with poor Lawson clearly about to breathe her last, you realise you'd better cut to the chase and ask a few pertinent questions.

But what should you ask her?

"I'm here alone at the moment. Is there a safe place to hide while I wait for help to arrive?" – If you want to ask Lawson this, turn to **077**.

"What do you think the Saturmeks want here, and is there anything I can do to stop them?" – If this is your choice of question then turn to **100**.

013

Silently and swiftly, you leave the Dorm and head back to the junction. Keeping a crouched posture, you scurry Southward down the Main Corridor towards the Airlock.

Turn to **078**.

014

"That is very... unfortunate," gasps Lawson. "Setting the Moonbase Self-Destruct System using just one of the Authorisation Codes is only for the direst of emergencies, when all hope is lost. You won't be able to set the countdown timer... detonation will be instant. I'm sorry, but I was hoping at least you would get out alive."

Now turn to **066**.

015

Suddenly rooted to the spot by abject terror, your mind reels as your worst nightmare becomes reality. Adrenaline floods your veins, causing your muscles to tremble and then tense. You grit your teeth and close your eyes to block out the sight of the metal monster advancing toward you.

"Focus," you think. "Be cool. Remember your training."

Something approximating calm envelopes you, allowing you, at least, clarity of thought and the courage to do whatever you decide is necessary. Opening your eyes, you see the Saturmek stood before you, its chest door is open, and its gun is levelled directly at you. There's something strangely impatient about the way it drums the floor with its leg-claws like fingers on a table top. Using your memory of your surroundings and only peripheral vision to confirm your mental map, you consider what should be your best course of action.

You are mere feet from the South Corridor, if you were to make a bolt for it you could be out of the Saturmek's line-of-fire in less than a second! Then, perhaps you could barricade yourself in the Dormitory... and maybe it has another exit?

Your only other option, it seems, is to surrender to this merciless killing-machine.

Which is it to be?

Will you risk a quick sprint to the Dorm and, perhaps, escape? Or would you rather surrender to the Saturmeks and hope they show you more mercy than they did the Moonbase crew?

If you think making a break for it gives you the best chance of survival, then turn to **092.**

If you feel that surrendering to the Saturmeks is the better option under the circumstances then you should turn to **182.**

016

You type the Authorisation Code into the terminal and press enter. The video screen momentarily goes blank and then the image returns as black text on an urgent yellow background.

```
Commander Rex King, you are now cleared to
initiate Sterilisation Protocol Alpha One.
```

Now add 20 points to your Savvy Score and turn to **143**.

017

You are vaguely aware of a cold, hard floor pressing against your back. Your head is thumping with what feels like a mild hangover, and your arms and legs throb with an itchy pins-and-needles feeling.

The sound of an Airlock Door slamming shut shakes you into full mental alertness, but your movements are sluggish and painful as you rise to your feet. You were definitely shot by a Saturmek and half-wonder if you're a now a ghost doomed to haunt Moonbase Shackleton for the rest of eternity. You recognise your surrounds; you're in the South Airlock.

You suddenly hear the trill electronic tones of a Saturmek coming from the other side of the door and listen intently as you creep numbly and unsteadily closer towards the porthole. You see the Green Drone Saturmek reporting to its Red Chief.

"The human attempted escape. I used a stun-ray to pacify it and brought it here for detention as ordered."

"You did well in resisting the urge to slay the vermin, our Science Officer would have been displeased as we might yet learn something from this erratic human," muses the Red Saturmek. "Now, secure the Airlock to ensure the prisoner cannot escape. Then immediately join us in the Operations Centre, we must continue our work on the artefact. This task still takes priority over anything else."

The Red Chief Saturmek heads Northward up the main corridor towards the Green Internal Airlock. You duck out of sight as the Drone swivels to face the door and verbally runs through a checklist;

"Airlock Door sealed and secured from this side. Internal lock mechanism over-ridden. It cannot be opened from the within by the prisoner."

Moments later you risk another glance through the porthole and see that both Saturmeks have now gone. The numbness in your limbs and the mussiness of your head is easing, so you can think clearly enough to start formulating an escape plan. Perhaps if you were to exit the Airlock via the other door and head out onto the Lunar surface, then...

To your dismay you see that the Emergency Evacuation Spacesuits that were hanging on hooks along the wall of the chamber have been reduced to charred and crumbling tatters.

"Out-smarted by the dratted Saturmek," you sigh heavily. "Suppose I should be grateful it didn't just kill me."

Add 10 points to your Savvy Score and turn to **183.**

018

"Yes," you reply gently. "I'm afraid Commander King didn't make it, but I do have his code."

"That's fortunate," gasps Lawson. "Setting the Moonbase self-destruct using both Rex's and my Authorisation Codes allows you to define the countdown timer. You can delay detonation for as much as four hours. I'm glad at least you'll get out alive."

Now turn to **185.**

019

"Why so comfy?" you ponder aloud. "The crew must've had to spend quite a lot of time in here for some reason."

Reminding yourself that time is not on your side you don't dwell too long on the strangely cosy Airlock interior and instead move to the centre of the room to consider your next move.

The Grey Airlock Door ahead of you beckons, and you'd like to know where it leads.

But the Spacesuits, hanging displayed in their own transparent acrylic case like a museum exhibit, also catch your eye. The suits look significantly more advanced, and much more like what you consider to be *proper* astronaut threads, than those you've previously seen on Shackleton.

You're curious about the contents of the drab, olive green lockers too, which have a militaristic look to them, and remind you of your own personal locker back at SItU HQ.

So, will you check out the Lockers first? To do this, please turn to **004**.

If you think examining the Spacesuits should be your first priority, turn to **115**.

Or, if you feel that the Grey Airlock Door deserves your immediate attention, then turn to **120**.

020

As you turn slowly on the spot, wondering in which direction you should head, your foot connects with something small and previously unnoticed on the floor, sending it skidding a good yard across the width of the corridor. For a moment you're startled, until you realise that it was an innocuous-looking white box that you accidentally kicked. You approach where it came to rest and, having stooped to pick it up, study the curious item.

The box appears to be made of plastic, about the size of a packet of twenty Silk Cut but with rounded corners, and mostly glossy white, but one of the wider surfaces is grey and has a cold, glassy feel to it. You see that there are four small recessed buttons running down one side, labelled POWER, MENU, REC and CAST. It must be some sort of cassette tape recorder, you reason, and so you press the POWER button.

The grey surface illuminates, and you realise it's a tiny television screen. Upon the screen is a message in neat, white text against a black background that reads:

MESSAGE NOT SENT. EXTRA-COM PORT ERROR. PRESS PLAY TO REVIEW, OR CAST TO RESEND.

You're not entirely sure you understand what the screen is trying to tell you, but you find the 'press play' bit very intriguing, particularly if there's a message to be read. You thumb the PLAY button.

The little screen is suddenly filled with a frantic video. An attractive woman, probably in her late-thirties, with a practical, short haircut, looks directly out of the picture at you. From the shake of the camera, you can tell she's running, and from the wideness of her eyes you can tell she's very alarmed.

"Mayday! Mayday!" exclaims the running woman. "This is Lieutenant Claire Lawson, Moonbase Shackleton. We're under attack. Saturmeks have invaded. Crew are all dead. Commander's missing... probably dead. Send Marines urgently! You gotta stop the Saturmeks!"

Now turn to **043.**

021

For a few brief moments you're tumbling, weightlessly, intangibly, and seemingly downwards, through a tunnel of twisting blue-green light, and then...

...you fall into Professor Wylie's arms.

"Easy, Hills, I got you," you immediately hear her say, in her calm, reassuring tone.

For a moment you can still hear the crackle of raw, angry vortex energy, and then a loud bang as sparks and smoke fountain from out of the salvaged time-travel engine like a roman candle. You and the Professor watch together as the Fugacious Spatial Vortex flickers and fades.

Professor Wylie grabs a small fire extinguisher from her lab-bench and crosses to the crackling, flaring machinery. With just a few skillfully-directed blasts of CO_2 she brings the sparking and smouldering under control.

"Such a pity," she mutters sulkily. "Took me half-an-hour of frantic work to reassemble the Berwyn Device and get it operational. Probably beyond salvaging now."

The Professor, frowning and pouting like a petulant child, then turns her attention to you.

"Are you alright, Hilary?" Wylie's query is brusque.

"Yeah, I'll be okay," you reply. "Professor, I was on..."

"A Moonbase, one hundred years in the future, I gathered as much from the view the vortex gave me of the airlock, Hills," interrupts the Professor. "You know, you should never have put the battery in that Temporal Condenser Circuit you were working on. I'd just started to tweak the settings in the very heart of the Tachyon Capacitor, you see, so once you'd turned on the Temporal Condenser, your fate was sealed."

You stare at the Professor, rather nonplussed by her explanation, and feeling very hurt and dismayed at her scalding. Professor Wylie sees the pain in your eyes and her expression immediately softens to one of earnest concern as she slowly approaches and, with a somewhat awkward demeanour, takes your hands in hers.

"You're quite ashen and – goodness gracious me! – you're trembling," she says softly.

"What d'you expect? I fell through time! To the Moon!" You try to sound angry, but with all you've been through it sounds more like a mewle of disbelief.

"Y'know... ah... actually..." stumbles Professor Wylie. "It's probably my fault you ended up there; my carelessness that caused the localised Temporal-Spatial Distortion. I'm sorry, Hills."

"Saturmeks," you reply, and are unsure what else to add until you blurt. "They're going to destroy the Earth!"

"Saturmeks? Really? Look, Hilary, I'm a bit fuzzy on physical laws of time, but I do know that whatever you've just witnessed, no matter how immediate and raw it seems to you, hasn't happened yet. In fact, it won't happen for a hundred years... if it happens at all."

The Professor's voice trails off with a heavy sigh. You can see by the distant look in her eyes, and the way she nervously twiddles her necklace, that the thought of the terrifying experience you underwent has just sunk in.

"Well, the Earth of here and now is under no imminent threat, that's the main thing," finishes the Professor disjointedly as she snaps out of her reverie. "Perhaps the return of the Saturmeks in the year 2074 is historical fact... er, future historical fact... that is to say, but it hasn't happened yet, and is a merely speculative future... but perhaps it will happen, and once it has happened, it will be fixed in history... ah... If you get my meaning."

You can't help but to smile at Professor Wylie's fumbling exposition, and with the lifting of your spirits you realize that you're home and safe.

"Why don't you try to explain it to me again, over a nice big mug of sweet tea in the NAAFI," you suggest warmly. "It's about time for elevensies."

Now turn to Epilogue at **200.**

022

Perhaps, if you were somehow able to clamber up to the giant's armrest, where you can see there's a control knob and switches, you might be able to... Yes! Oh, but how to get up there? It must be forty-odd feet high.

You cross the floor hastily to one of the many tripod-mounted floodlights. Giving a determined tug on the very lengthy power cables, you delight in seeing it uncouple from the generator many yards distant. You bound back over to the feet of the giant, your make-shift grappling hook in hand and an abundance of improvised climbing rope trailing after.

Now turn to **164**.

023

The Saturmek, its gun still levelled at your chest, scuttles a few feet backwards.

"You will exit the room. Now!"

You do as your told of course, because defiance would likely be met with instant death, and step cautiously out from the Stores and into the corridor.

"You will walk ahead of me and follow my directions," orders the Saturmek.

Timidly you comply; leading the Drone down the corridor with your arms raised.

You reach the junction.

023

"Halt," demands the Saturmek. "Now that we are in a less confined space, you will turn to face me."

Getting a better look at your captor now, you see that its metal casing is spattered liberally with dark red gouts of human blood.

"I presume you're the merciless brute who butchered the crew," you mutter.

Now turn to **008.**

024

As abruptly as it started, the weightless, upward tumbling through swirling light and breathless silence ends with an ignominious bump as your backside connects with a cold floor. Although shaken by your journey, you immediately leap to your feet alert, but the small, white, all-but empty room you find yourself in clearly offers no immediate threat. You take a pause and, still feeling bewildered, look about your surroundings.

"What the heck did your crazy contraption do, Professor?" you mutter, as your eyes fall upon a row of day-glow orange overalls hanging from coat-hooks along one wall, below which is a simple bench. "And where am I? This seems to be a space-age cloak room."

You take a closer look at the overalls; they're large, baggy garments made from some sort of canvas-like material, ribbed at the elbows and knees, and with a yellow plastic box, about the size of a house brick but very lightweight, affixed to the left breast from which thin pipes run around the torso and down the limbs. Thick gloves are attached to the sleeve cuffs, and likewise the legs end in chunky boots. The oversized neck opening is stiff and has a distinct lip at the top. The upper arms of each sleeve incorporate a deep mesh-material pocket, each containing a metal canister roughly the size and shape of a milk bottle. You ponder the purpose of these suits briefly, until you notice what are obviously Space Helmets stowed neatly beneath the bench.

On the opposite wall, neatly stencilled in a large, precise typeface, are the words:

Airlock South.

The remaining two walls of this narrow chamber, which is no wider than a London Tube carriage, and half as long, are almost entirely taken up by large, round, hefty-looking bright orange bulkhead-style doors.

The door to the North end of the room contains a small porthole which looks out onto a long, brightly-lit but featureless corridor. Above the porthole is affixed an official-looking plaque which, you note with a measured mixture of apprehension and disbelief, reads:

Welcome to Moonbase Shackleton, British Lunar Scientific Research Facility. Established: 2073 AD. Resident Crew: 08

The identical orange bulkhead door to the South end of the room also contains a porthole, but whatever lies beyond this door isn't immediately obvious from where you stand and all you see is darkness. You approach the door to peer through the inches-thick glass and find yourself looking out onto an open, grey, barren and slightly undulating dusty plain. Hanging in the inky black sky is a luminous globe which you immediately recognise as Earth.

"Yep, I've travelled into the future, and I'm on the flippin' Moon!" you sigh, deciding to take all this strangeness in your stride, just as you know Professor Wylie would.

Your keen eye then spies something glint on the Lunar surface, and you press your nose against the cold window, squinting to bring whatever it might be into sharper focus. There, a few hundred yards distant, you see an upturned wheeled vehicle, bloated rubber wheels spinning impotently against the black sky, jets of gas venting from its chassis, and burst of yellow sparks intermittently lighting up the scene of the accident. It looks like it might explode at any moment!

You let out a gasp when you spot, a short distance from the smashed Moon-buggy, lying motionless in the grey dust of the chill Lunar desert, the buggy's spacesuited driver. Looking to you every bit like an unconscious *Michelin Man*, the prone figure is wearing what you consider to be a *proper* spacesuit; nothing like the flimsy orange affairs hanging on hooks in here. Your immediate impression is that this person crashed their Moon-buggy a short time ago, given that the engine is still running, and they're in need of help.

What should you do?

Will you do as Professor Wylie ordered; remain exactly where you are until she comes to the rescue? If you chose to do as you were told, turn to **086.**

Or should you venture out of the North Airlock Door, which will take you into the corridors of the Moonbase, hoping to find someone who can help the crashed Moon-buggy driver? To do this, turn to **034.**

Or do you dare dress yourself in one of the Orange Spacesuits, and head immediately out onto the Lunar surface to rescue the helpless astronaut yourself? To choose this action, turn to **075.**

025

The lighting in the chamber dims as the amber beacon above the door illuminates, flooding the room in orange pulsing light. To your immense dismay a warning klaxon also sounds.

"Shush, damn it!" you hiss, because the futility of scalding a computer-controlled bulkhead door escapes you at this particular moment. "I hope the Saturmeks can't hear this!"

The video screen on the door changes from blue to red and the text now reads:

CHAMBER DECOMPRESSION INITIATED.
DECOMPRESSING... 60.

The on-screen digit promptly changes to 59, then 58, 57, as it counts down the one-minute-long decompression procedure.

You're wearing a Spacesuit, borrowed from a member of the Moonbase crew, aren't you? Aren't you?!

The last three digits of her Crew Registration Number is the reference to which you **should now turn.** *

If you are not wearing a Spacesuit, and therefore do not know Minodora Atasiei's Crew Registration Number, you must turn to **005.**

For example, if the Crew Registration Number of the owner of your borrowed Spacesuit is 1123456789 then you would turn to reference 789.

026

You allow a whistle to escape you pensively pursed lips and hope you've remembered Mino's lengthy Crew Registration Number correctly, because it's kinda tricky to see her name-tag now that you're actually wearing her Spacesuit! Your fingers tap the numbered keys in the correct sequence as asterisks appear on the screen with each number entered. With the tenth and final digit typed in, you take a step back and wait with baited breath.

Nothing happens.

You wait a few interminable moments more, then peer at the screen again; your string of asterisks remains on the display beneath the words ENTER LOGIN.

"Enter?" You mutter, somewhat nonplussed by this futuristic keyboard. You then see a key on the right-hand side of the keypad which contains a diagram of an arrow bending back on itself, rather like the return key on your electric typewriter back at SItU Headquarters. You take a deep breath, choose to trust your intuition, and press it...

The screen clears momentarily, and then some fresh text is displayed:

LOGIN REJECTED. CREW MEMBER MINODORA ATASIEI, YOU ARE NOT AUTHORISED TO OPERATE THIS AIRLOCK. PLEASE REFER TO YOUR DUTY SENIOR.

"Bugger it!" you curse aloud.

You're confusing Moonbase Crew Registration Numbers for Authorisation Codes, and they're clearly not the same thing. Flippin' futuristic red tape! You need to rethink.

You must now turn back to **162.**

027

Professor Wylie looks down to her bowl, picks up the spoon again and prods idly at the cooling suet.

"You know the Saturmeks, Hills," she says softly. "They're ruthless murderers, and you showed great courage in both thought and deed when you went up against a squad of them alone."

"You did tell me to stay put," you add. "But I couldn't just sit there and wait for you, what with all that was going on."

"I did tell you to stay put, yes," replies the Professor, slowly looking up from her pudding to meet your eyes with a mischievous smile. "But... Earth threatened with utter destruction, a squad of Saturmeks running amok, the Moonbase crew dead or dying; and at great personal risk you took it upon yourself to save the World. That's my Hilary!"

"It's good to be home safe, Professor," you smile.

"Relieved to have you home safe, Hills," returns the Professor with a broad beam. "And it's also fascinating to learn that the Saturmeks are still at large out there in space. We had hoped the germ bombs devised back in '97 had finished them off for good, but always suspected that there might be a few survivors that escaped. It's a pity that current rocket technology doesn't allow us to take the fight to them, but at least it seems we have decades to prepare."

"I'm pretty certain there were no Saturmek survivors this time," you say.

"Although," ventures Professor Wylie, cautiously. "Using an atomic bomb to stop just four of them? It does seem a bit drastic, Hills, like using a sledgehammer to crack a walnut."

"That's exactly what I thought," you reply, feeling a little crestfallen at the Professor's hint of disapproval. "But I had to use what was at hand. The Saturmeks had to be stopped!"

"Well, quite," sighs the Professor, but then her demeanour suddenly softens again. "To think; it was... er... will be my very own assistant who foils the Saturmeks on that fateful future day and saves Earth from utter annihilation. Well done, Hills. I'm proud of you. You showed – will show? – tremendous courage. Goodness, it's a hard job to get your head around the tenses when talking about something *you-will-do, but have-already-done* in the future!"

"Yeah," you reply, trying to shrug off your melancholy.

"Professor..." interrupts a familiar voice. You both look over to see Sir Clive Browne striding towards your table.

"Top of the morning to you, Sir Clive," greets Professor Wylie.

"Good morning, Vyvian," replies Browne. "Looking a little glum there, Hills."

"I just detonated an atomic bomb on the Moon to kill four Saturmeks," you reply with some self-reproach.

"What's that?" Sir Clive raises an eyebrow at the cryptic comment. "Oh, I see; some sort of theoretical role-play exercise you're doing?"

"Something like that, Sir Clive, yes," replies the Professor, giving you a friendly wink.

"Saturmeks on the Moon, eh?" muses Sir Clive. "That's our sovereign territory! Yes, a well-aimed warhead would put a stop to those blighters' shenanigans with minimum fuss. Good choice, Hills, exactly what I would've ordered."

Professor Wylie flashes you a cheeky gurn; eyebrows arched, eyes crossed, the tip of her tongue sticking out the corner of her mouth. You can't help but to laugh.

"Something funny?" asks the nonplussed Browne.

"No, Sir Clive," replies the Professor, straightening her features and looking directly to her superior. "Well, what demands are about to make on my precious time now?"

"What? Oh, yes," blusters Sir Clive. "Strange lights were spotted in the sky over Stonehenge last night, and this morning the Heel Stone was discovered to be missing."

"Intriguing," mutters Wylie, and falls silent for a moment before she starts to murmur her thoughts to herself. "Although, I doubt it's actually missing. I mean, who'd be able to move a thirty-five-ton lump of sarsen stone overnight? Where would they move it to? And why? Highly improbable."

"Vyvian?" prompts Sir Clive.

"Sir Clive," announces the Professor, snapping out of her reverie. "I strongly suspect the stone's still in place, but is dimensionally cloaked. It's been rendered invisible, so to speak."

"You'll take a look at it, then," replies Sir Clive, his tone, as always with the Professor, being a practiced mixture of polite request and authoritative demand.

"At once, Sir Clive," agrees the Professor with enthusiasm as she rises from her chair. "Coming, Hills?"

You jump to your feet, raring to go.

"Ditch the spacesuit, and bring some chalk, a ball of string, and a couple of strong magnets, Hills," calls back Professor Wylie as she breezes out of the room.

"Never a dull moment, Sir Clive," you say, and then you chase after the Professor on your way to a new adventure.

The End.

028

You follow the West Passageway to the Storeroom. The door, you find, is indeed made of steel – not lighter alloys or plastics like the others around the Moonbase – as is the wall into which it is embedded. It's secured with a simple sliding bolt, which moves with oiled ease. You enter the Storeroom.

Lights detect your presence and flicker into life, revealing a chamber which is large, well-lit and well ordered. It's constructed from steel plate; the walls, floor and ceiling are bare metal, with visible welding seams and hefty rivets. Along each wall are rows of shelving units, each tidily loaded with provisions and equipment.

The contents of the shelving are mostly scientific-looking items at one end; circuit-boards, things that might be hand-held computers, equipment with lenses which are possibly telescopes or microscopes, perplexing technology of the future you can't possibly hope to recognise.

Another shelf unit contains paraphernalia you'd mostly associate with construction or, more likely, archaeology; drills, picks, torches, sealable plastic tubs, battery-packs, light-poles... but, you note forlornly, nothing that might be used as a weapon against Saturmeks. You do take a neat-looking penlight torch, testing it and finding its tiny lightbulb throws a quite brilliant beam; you'll make a gift of it to Professor Wylie, she loves gadgets like this.

Against another wall are shelves of food-stuffs; a supermarket in miniature. You can see protein packs, bags of grains, cereals and rice, a sack of teabags, shrink-wrapped dried cured meats, plastic tubs of fruits in syrup, and many sundry other items. A large plastic keg, holding what you guess to be hundreds of gallons of water, sits on a sturdy tripod. The plumbing work that leads to and from it suggest that this is a water recycling machine.

You're not thirsty, and most definitely lack any appetite right now.

Now turn to **098**.

029

Again, you glance about your surroundings, anxious that time is not your friend today.

If you haven't already, you might choose to check – or double-check – the drab, olive green lockers set against the wall. To do this, turn to **004.**

Or you might want to cross the room to that bulky-looking Grey Airlock Door at the East end of the chamber. If this is your choice, turn to **120.**

030

The Green Airlock door is a simpler affair than the South Orange one you arrived at earlier. On the door is riveted a plaque which reads:

Operations Area.

Authorised Personnel Only Beyond This Point.

You see that the Airlock Door can be opened by a simple left–right locking wheel, and you expect that it's designed, like a submarine's bulkhead, to be secured in a hurry to isolate the Operations Area of the Moonbase from the

Living Quarters in the event of a hull-breach or similar emergency.

Above the wheel is a porthole, which you cautiously peer through. You see that the corridor you currently stand in continues to run North for about fifty yards, terminating in a set of white double doors marked *Operations Centre*. About halfway up the corridor is a crossroads junction with secondary, smaller corridors leading off to the left and right; repeating the layout of the Living Quarters you're currently in.

Now turn to **074.**

031

Mr. and Mrs. Hills – and Nanny – raised their only child to be bright, brave and independent... but you know that if a squad of Saturmeks and their genocidal plan are to be foiled, then you can't do it alone and need back-up!

You glance at your watch. Half-an-hour, the Professor had promised you from the other end of her Time Tornado, and you see that nearly thirty minutes have passed since you first found yourself on the Moon.

It's time to go!

Now turn to **061.**

032

As you take a few slow, cautious steps into the silence and darkness, a strong tang of ozone fills your nostrils. The lights in the room flicker on; a motion sensor has detected you and now illuminates the canteen.

You gasp, and are forced to stifle a yelp at the awful sight that meets you; there are six crew members here... all are dead. That explains the whiff of ozone which hangs in the air; energy weapons were fired in here a short time ago.

You compose yourself and survey the scene with forensic detachment. What's evident is that this was the work of a Saturmek, and it was brutally efficient in dispatching its prey; bursting into the canteen and opening fire swiftly on the unsuspecting crew, causing shock, confusion and outright terror.

Three of the crew are still sat at the table where they breakfasted, slumped lifeless with horrifyingly anguished expressions on their faces. Two others lie nearby, their bodies contorted through muscular spasm into the undignified postures of pain-wracked demise. The sixth victim, a blonde woman of petite build who looks to be no older than you, appears to be the only crew member who had any time to react; she put up a fight, possibly because flight was no option. You deduce that she picked up a chair and set about battering her assailant with it. Her body is criss-crossed with countless deep, bloody gouges that look to have been inflicted by glancing blows from a chainsaw or something similar. Hers was not the quick death of her colleagues, and you reflect that the brutal Saturmek could, presumably, have shot her at any time during their tussle, but instead chose to torment her with this death of a thousand cuts.

032 - 033

The Saturmeks, you now fully appreciate, are every bit as brutal, sadistic, and inhuman as the historical accounts of 1879 relate.

There are six dead crew here and the seventh, as you've already seen, lies outside the Moonbase in his Spacesuit. You wonder where the eighth can be.

You have no desire to remain in this ghastly place, and there's nothing more to learn here, so you turn on your heels and exit via the way you came in.

Add 10 points to your Savvy Score and turn to **064.**

033

You take the two hemispherical mines from your satchel and study them with grim determination. You have no desire to die, but the Saturmeks' planet-killing genocidal plan must be stopped. Here alone, you can see no other option but to risk your life to save billions.

You decide to mine the Ancient Obelisk Artefact. If you've understood half of what you've overheard correctly then this stone needle is, quite literally, the ignition key to start the Moon's engines. Destroying it should permanently foil the Saturmek plan.

You observe that the Saturmeks have become more animated, gesturing with their mechanical limbs and swivelling their head-domes. You've got to stay cool, be patient, and wait for your opportunity to sneak from under cover.

You watch as the Saturmeks then scuttle across to a large bank of computer consoles to the North side of the room.

The mechanical fiends all have their backs to you and so, realising that this might be your only chance to sneak out, you decide to make your move.

Now turn to **130**.

034

Having decided that getting help will be best course of action, you approach the Airlock Door wondering how to go about opening it.

Suddenly, in the middle of the room, a shimmering ball of light appears accompanied by a worryingly familiar ethereal crackle of raw, angry energy. No bigger than a tennis ball, the ghostly orb looks to be spinning at an incredible velocity as it phases through umpteen shades of blue. The mysterious sphere suddenly swells to the size of a football, and then morphs rapidly into something more conical in shape, still spinning wildly it now disturbingly resembles a tornado. Pressing yourself into a corner, you keep as much distance between you and the phantasmal whirling dervish as you can, but the fearsome, tapering column of electric-blue light creeps inch-by-inch toward you – as if it's seeking you out in a game of blind-man's bluff – and then it topples. Extremely unnerved, and daring not to move a muscle, you're now staring into the wide maw of a horizontal tornado of swirling, spinning plasma and lightning!

A crackling, echoing voice, faint and barely distinct, whispers from deep within the vaporous funnel...

"Hilary Hills? Can you hear me? It's Professor Wylie."

"Professor!" you call back, feeling your spirits soar. "I can hear you... just about."

"I've got the Berwyn Device working, and it's located you! I managed to combine the Temporal Condenser Circuit with the Tachyon Capacitor to create a Fugacious Spatial Vortex from me to you. That's what you're looking at now, and how I'm able talk to you. I know where you are, Hills, and I can bring you home!"

"How do I get back, Professor? Is this tornado-thing the *Phew-gaseous Special Vortex?*"

"Yes, but I'm going to have to make the passageway considerably bigger before you can enter it. Shouldn't take too long. Half an hour should do it. Hold tight, Hills, just stay exactly where you are."

"But, Professor, there's..."

The funnel of swirling blue light crackles and judders, then suddenly it distorts into a doughnut shape.

"Confound it!" you hear Professor Wylie curse as the Fugacious Spatial Vortex turns a dark purple hue before blinking out of existence.

"Half an hour should do it." you mull over the Professor's words to yourself. "Thirty minutes is a long time to spend sat on my rear doing nothing!"

You decide you have enough time to *recce* the Moonbase, and so turn your attention back to the airlock door.

Turn to **037.**

035

You take the two hemispherical mines from your satchel and study them with grim determination. You have no desire to die, but the Saturmek's planet-killing genocidal plan must be stopped. Here alone, you can see no other option but to risk your life to save billions.

Recalling the Operational Directions you browsed earlier, you decide to booby-trap the doors. Using the self-adhesive strips, you attached a mine to each door and then play out the trip-cord and attach it to the adjacent doorframe. You then prime each mine.

You have no idea how powerful the explosives are, but assume they were used by the Moonbase Archaeologists for blasting Lunar rock during their excavations, so you guess they must be pretty potent. Sooner or later, you know that the Saturmeks will exit the Operations Centre via the swinging doors, the wires will be tripped and... *Boom!* Hopefully the blast will destroy the Saturmeks, and probably demolish some of the infrastructure of the base, causing catastrophic decompression and a great deal of carnage.

Add 15 points to your Savvy Score and then turn to **171.**

036

The Green Airlock door is a far simpler affair than the South Orange one you arrived at earlier. On the door is riveted a plaque which reads:

Operations Area.

Authorised Personnel Only Beyond This Point.

You see that the Airlock Door can be opened by a simple left–right locking wheel, and you suspect it's designed to be secured in a hurry to isolate the Operations Area of the Moonbase from the Living Quarters in the event of a hull-breach or similar emergency, like a submarine's bulkhead.

Above the wheel is a porthole, which you cautiously peer through. You see that the corridor you are in continues to run Northwards for about fifty yards, terminating in a set of white double doors marked *Operations Centre*. About halfway up the corridor is a crossroads junction with secondary, smaller corridors leading off to the left and right; repeating the layout of the Living Quarters you're currently in.

Will you open the Green Airlock Door and pass into the Operations Area of Moonbase Shackleton?

If so, turn to **074.**

Or, if you feel you might have missed something, would you prefer to retrace your steps about twenty-five yards back to the junction?

To choose this action, turn to **198.**

037

The Airlock door is a large, circular affair with a rather complicated-looking locking handle mechanism located just below its portal window. Stencilled onto the door are clearly-written instructions and pictograms of how to operate it, and so you follow the simple three-step guide.

You turn the green dial on the left of the door from 'X' to 'O', then press the green stud-button on the right of the door when it lights up, and finally pull the red handle, located on the central lock itself, downwards.

The hefty door swings outward, driven by entirely silent motors, and you step cautiously out into the corridor.

Now turn to **045**.

038

You and Professor Wylie wander nonchalantly down the corridors, heading in the general direction the Professor's lab.

"He thought I was a coward, until you stuck up for me. I got off lightly, didn't I?" you say, and it's more of a statement than a question.

"A fortnight's paid holiday? I'd say you did!" Professor Wylie replies with a chuckle.

"But I've got to see a shrink!" you exclaim. "Oh, the indignity!"

"Nothing wrong in that," reassures the Professor. "You'll like Pete – Doctor Gardner – he's a nice chap. I've had need of his auspices in the past. He likes to practice his counselling down the Red Lion over a pint of Guinness and a cigar."

"Blimey," you coo. "I'll look forward to that, then."

And so, as you and the Professor continue to amble down the labyrinthine corridors, in the kind of comfortable and understanding silence that only good friends can share, you once again reflect on the events the day so far, and decide that if you could live this morning all over again, you'd probably do things quite differently.

The End.

039

The mechanical fiends are thoroughly engrossed in their studying of the Obelisk, probing it with their mechanical appendages and having some sort of discussion, but mostly they seem to be talking excitedly over each other. You know what the Saturmeks are saying concerning this ancient alien relic must be vitally important, but you can't clearly hear what they're talking about.

You think it might be possible to quietly slip into the room unnoticed, but judging from your limited view of the Operations Centre, the room's open-plan layout and transparent walls seem to offer no obvious hiding places.

Will you risk slipping into the Operations Centre to spy on the Saturmeks, hoping to get a clearer idea of what they're planning? If so, turn to **051.**

Or should you remain eavesdropping outside while you think up a different and less blatantly dangerous course of action? To do this, turn to **062.**

040

You allow a whistle to escape your pensively pursed lips and hope that you've remembered the late Lieutenant Claire Lawson's lengthy code correctly. Your fingers tap the numbered keys in the correct sequence as asterisks appear on the screen with each number entered. With the eleventh and final digit typed in, you take a step back and wait with baited breath.

Nothing happens.

You wait for a few interminable moments more, then peer at the screen again; your string of asterisks remains on the display beneath the words ENTER LOGIN.

"Enter?" You mutter, somewhat nonplussed by this futuristic keyboard. Then you see a key on the right-hand side of the keypad which contains a diagram of an arrow bending back on itself... rather like the return key on your electric typewriter back at SItU Headquarters. You take a deep breath, chose to trust your intuition, and press it.

The screen momentarily goes blank, then fresh text is displayed:

LOGIN AUTHORISED.

THANK YOU, LIEUTENANT LAWSON.

"Thank you, Claire," you say aloud, knowing that some part of her remains with you in spirit. "It really was as easy as Pi."

Now turn to **025.**

041

Summoning up all of your courage, and feeling a steely determination to protect precious planet Earth from the abominable and genocidal Saturmeks at any cost, you silently and swiftly exit the Dorm and head back to the junction. Keeping a crouched posture and staying close to the wall, you scurry the short distance Northwards up the main corridor towards the Green Airlock.

Now turn to **030.**

042

As the Green Saturmek approaches you, a hinged panel on the right of its body opens and a telescopic limb emerges from the cavity; a cruel-looking mechanical claw on the long, flexible shaft snatches at you, connecting with your upper right arm and taking an uncomfortably firm grip. The Drone then manhandles you unceremoniously all the way down the central corridor towards the South Airlock.

Once at the Orange Airlock, your captor frees you from its vice-like grip. It orders you to open the door and enter. Grateful to still be alive, you obey.

Now turn to **011**.

043

Lieutenant Lawson's next blurted words are drowned out by the *vizzzz* of an energy weapon firing. She screams in pain as the picture spins wildly; you realise that it was this very gizmo she'd been using to make her mayday call, and that you're standing in the same corridor she was running down when she was shot.

You continue to listen as the video playback, now showing just the corridor's ceiling, is reduced to a disturbing series of shallow, gasping breaths. Then, the message falls silent, and the image on the screen returns to white text on a black background:

`PRESS CAST TO SEND.`

"Saturmeks?" you mumble, utterly horrified by everything you've just seen and heard.

043

Every schoolkid knows about the Saturmeks; the race of war-mongering mechanical creatures from outer space, who invaded Earth in the year 1897. Dubbed *Martians* by the authorities of the time, it's since been established that their origins lay somewhere beyond our neighbouring Red Planet, and that they'd simply used Mars as a staging post. The Saturmek hordes stormed our planet with breathtaking ferocity; turning cities into wastelands and slaughtering hundreds of thousands of people. When conventional means of defence proved largely ineffectual, both military and scientific leaders agreed to unleash their last resort; an aggressive campaign of germ warfare. The Saturmeks occupying our planet fell foul of the virulent man-made contagion and died in their masses but, as they did so, they broadcast an oath of revenge across the airwaves. From that day, Earth has been ever vigilant, but no human has set eyes on a Saturmek since then...

...until now, it seems. Whenever exactly now is.

You realise every bit as much as Lawson did that Earth is in terrible danger now the Saturmeks have returned. You wonder what became of the Lieutenant's body, but don't dwell on the matter. Hoping this little fag-packet device will manage to transmit the mayday now, you press the CAST button on the device.

```
MESSAGE NOT SENT. EXTRA-COM PORT ERROR. PRESS
PLAY TO REVIEW, OR CAST TO RESEND.
```

You let the useless futuristic videophone thing fall to the floor, and long sigh escapes your lips. You notice you're trembling a little, and you instinctively stoop as you look about and reconsider your situation.

Now turn to **072.**

044

Professor Wylie looks down to her bowl, picks up the spoon again and prods idly at the custard-drenched suet.

"You know the Saturmeks, Hills," she says softly. "They're ruthless murderers, and you showed great courage going up against a squad of them alone."

"You did tell me to stay put," you add. "But I had to try, sorry."

"I did, yes," replies the Professor as she slowly looks up from pudding and meets your eyes with a mischievous smile. "But... Earth threatened with utter destruction, a squad of Saturmeks running amok, the Moonbase crew dead or dying; you took a great personal risk in the hope of making a difference, and that's what counts."

"It's good to be home safe, Professor," you smile.

"Relieved to have you home safe, Hills," returns the Professor with a broad beam. "And it's also fascinating to learn that the Saturmeks are still at large out there in space. We had hoped the germ bombs devised back in '97 had finished them off for good, but always suspected that there might be a few survivors that escaped. It's a pity that current rocket technology doesn't allow us to take the fight to them, but at least it seems we have decades to prepare."

"Professor Wylie..." interrupts a familiar voice. You both look over to see Sergeant Cox hurrying to your table.

"Good morning, Sergeant," greets the Professor. "Well, what demands is Sir Clive about to make on my precious time now?"

"He wants you to head down to Falmouth immediately," replies Cox. "Apparently some boat called *Atalanta* has just sailed into port."

"*Atalanta*? That wouldn't be the HMS *Atalanta* which went missing without a trace in 1880, would it?"

"Er, yes, that'll be the one," replies Cox sheepishly.

"How very intriguing," the Professor mutters to herself. "A possible side-effect of my dalliances with time travel technology this morning, perhaps? No. Well, maybe…"

"Beg pardon?" interrupts Cox.

"I said; I suppose I'd better get down there," announces the Professor as she rises from the table.

You jump to your feet, raring to go.

"Hills," adds Professor Wylie. "My lab is in an awful mess, I'd like you to have it ship-shape and Bristol-fashion by the time I get back, please."

"Bristol what?" grumbles the Sergeant, nonplussed. "I told her Falmouth, didn't I, Hills?"

"How about grabbing a broom and giving me a hand?" you suggest to Sergeant Cox as you both watch Professor Wylie breeze out of the room and on her way to a new adventure.

The End.

045

The lengthy corridor which stretches out ahead of you is featureless and purely utilitarian, with no decor or personal touches to give you an insight into the kind of people who occupy this sterile place. It's also quite wide; you could probably drive an HGV lorry down it without brushing the sides or ceiling.

You see that the corridor terminates with another sturdy Airlock Door about fifty yards ahead of you. Halfway down the corridor is a crossroads junction with secondary, smaller corridors leading off to the left and right.

This is unknown territory, and you're not certain how the occupants of Moonbase Shackleton are going to take your unexpected trespass, so you resist the urge to call out a hearty *Hello, anybody there?* in case you cause alarm, and instead walk swiftly but quietly up the length of the passage.

Your brisk strides promptly bring you to the junction where a narrower East-West passage intersects the Main Corridor. The Moonbase remains eerily silent as you pause, look about yourself, and consider your options.

Turn to **020**.

046

You've heard enough to know that Earth is in the most terrible and imminent peril! But what can you do? You need a few moments to think... preferably somewhere safer than here.

Still crouched low, you scurry the fifty yards Southwards down the corridor, back to the junction, and take a sharp left to hide around the corner of the East Corridor.

You allow yourself a little time to calm your nerves, chew a stick of peppermint gum, and consider your next move.

Now turn to **055**.

047

You type the Authorisation Code into the terminal and press enter. The video screen goes blank momentarily, and then the image returns as black text on an urgent yellow background.

```
Lieutenant Claire Lawson, you are now cleared
to initiate Sterilisation Protocol Alpha One.
```

Now add 20 points to your Savvy Score and turn to **143**.

048

You perch yourself down on the bench, prepared to quietly sit-out the next half-hour until the Professor's electric blue Time Tornado makes its reappearance. You reason that you're a stranger in a strange place and at an even stranger time, so it's best not to get tangled up in any of the goings-on here. Besides, you and Professor Wylie have previously theorised about the delicate nature of time having both read Bradbury's *The Sound of Thunder*.

You are suddenly rattled from your self-reflection by an eerily inhuman electronic voice just the other side of the North door.

"What the...!" you silence your involuntarily gasp as you instinctively slip from the bench, adopting a crouched stance, and scurry towards the door. Pressing yourself up against the airlock door so as not to be seen from outside, you take a deep breath and summon up the courage to take a quick peek through the porthole window. The chilling sight that meets your eyes confirms your very worst fears; in the corridor, positioned with its back to you and barely a few feet from the door behind which you now cower, is unmistakably a Saturmek!

Every schoolkid knows about the Saturmeks; a race of war-mongering mechanical creatures from outer space, who invaded Earth in the year 1897. Dubbed *Martians* by the authorities of the time, it's since been established that their origins lay somewhere beyond our neighbouring Red Planet, and that they'd simply used Mars as a staging post. The Saturmek hordes stormed our planet with breathtaking ferocity; turning cities into wastelands and slaughtering hundreds of thousands of people. When conventional means of defence proved largely ineffectual,

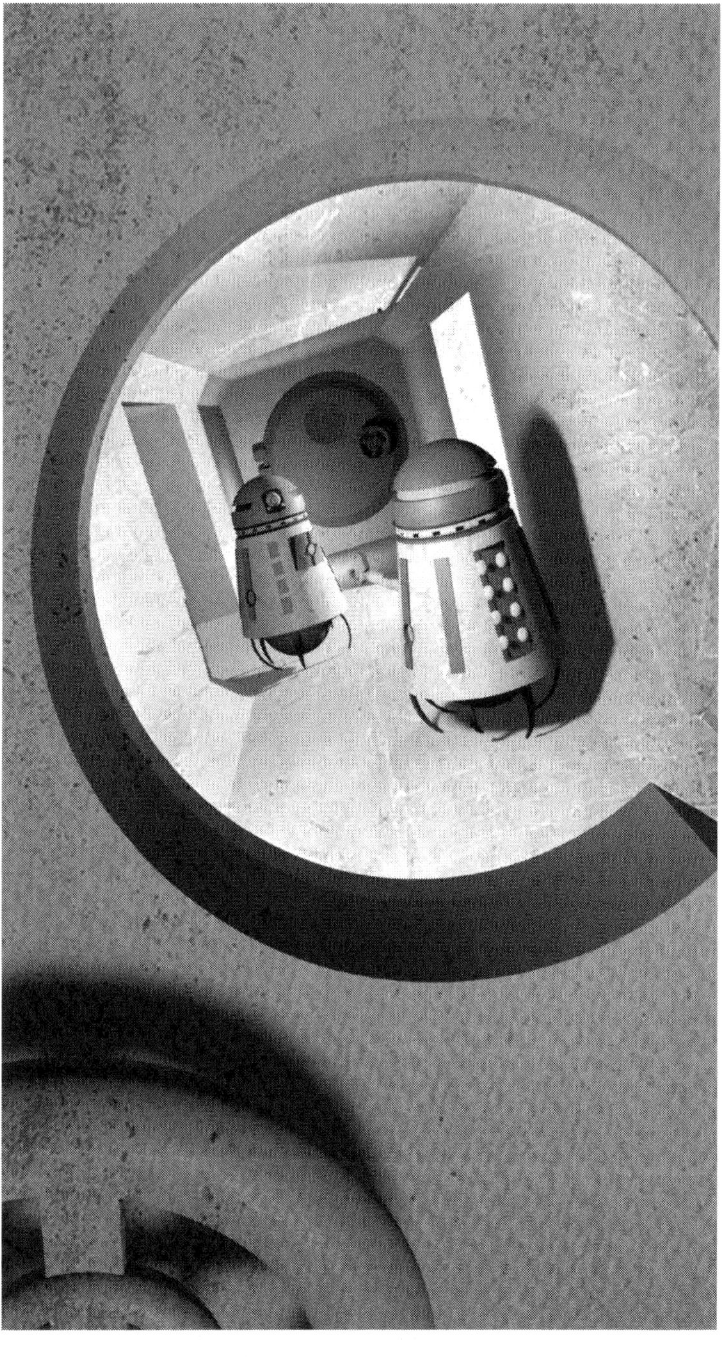

both military and scientific leaders agreed to unleash their last resort; an aggressive campaign of germ warfare. The Saturmeks occupying our planet fell foul of the virulent man-made contagion and died in their masses but, as they did so, they broadcast an oath of revenge across the airwaves. From that day, the people of Earth have been ever watchful and vigilant, but no human has set eyes on a Saturmek since then...

...until now.

"A red one," you mutter to yourself with sour dismay. "Command rank."

A second Saturmek, its drab green casing battered and battle-scarred, enters the corridor from an adjoining one to the left and approaches its superior. You duck down, not daring to continue to spy through the porthole in fear of being spotted, but continue to listen intently.

Now turn to **196.**

049

You carefully key the first Authorisation Code into the terminal and press enter. The blinking cursor reappears beneath the string of numbers you typed, awaiting more data. You hastily enter the second of the Codes.

The video screen momentarily goes blank and then the image returns as black text on a yellow background.

```
Commander Rex King and Lieutenant Claire
Lawson, you are jointly cleared to initiate
Sterilisation Protocol Alpha One.
```

049

```
Please define the desired countdown time to
detonation.
```

You know the maximum allowed time is 240 minutes, but that feels unnecessarily long, and so type 15 and press *enter*. A quarter of an hour should be time enough, you hope, to get back to the Orange Airlock and rendezvous with Professor Wylie.

A small and hitherto unseen panel to the right of the keyboard slides open to reveal a big, red button.

```
Priming of fusion-boosted fission devices will
commence when activation button is pressed.

A data report will be generated and
transmitted to Earth Command.

Priming Procedure and Data Transmission takes
approximately 10 seconds.

Detonation then follows at the user-defined
period of: 15 minutes.

Please press the activation button now.
```

You don't hesitate to hit the button. In a quarter of an hour Moonbase Shackleton and the Saturmeks that seized it will be history, and then Earth – and every soul upon her – will be safe.

The text on the screen renews:

```
Gathering Data.

Transmitting data.

Arming fusion-boosted fission devices.

Devices armed.

Detonation in:   14:59... 14:58... 14:57
```

A final message appears beneath the countdown:

```
Sterilisation Protocol Alpha One can be
aborted at any time by pressing the ESC key.
```

You grasp the keypad with both gauntleted hands and rip it from its housing. You smash the device repeatedly against the corner of the nearby desk, then drop the battered technology to the floor and stamp on it until only fragments remain.

"Nobody's going to be pressing that flippin' *esc* key," you mutter.

Now add a critically massive 99 points to your Savvy Score and turn **126**.

050

You must formulate a plan, Hilary, and be quick about it!

Are you, by any chance, carrying any explosive Blasting Ordnance?

If you are, turn to **146**.

If you do not any such explosives on your person, then you must turn to **010**.

051

You summon up every ounce of courage and then, on your hands and knees, slowly push the door open, just a crack at first, then a little more. Keeping low, you dare to poke your head around the door for a peek.

The four Saturmeks are gathered around the Stone Needle in the centre of the rotunda room. Sucker-cup appendages are extended from cavities in their bodies to touch the mysterious artefact, their head-domes occasionally twitch a little, but generally the Saturmeks are motionless and silent. You get the impression they're studying the artefact intently, deep in concentration.

No more than fifteen feet from the door is a bank of computer terminals, looking for all the world like a row of filing cabinets with knobs, dials and blinking lights on them. Ideal to hide behind, you reckon! Still on all fours, you slip quietly into the Operations Centre and scurry the short distance to terminals.

Now turn to **007**.

052

Suddenly, as if in response to your whispered plea, that longed-for shimmering ball of light reappears in the middle of the room, accompanied by a thunderous roar of crackling, raw energy.

From cricket ball, through football, the light phases and pulses. Then it grows rapidly to a size that fills half the chamber as it morphs into the now-welcome sight of a horizontal tornado of swirling, spinning plasma and lightning. A familiar voice, as clear as a bell, issues from deep within the ethereal funnel…

"Hills! I can see you," says Professor Wylie, with relief evident in her voice. "Can you see me?"

You peer into the Fugacious Spatial Vortex, having to squint against the harshness of the electric-blue light, and there, in a giddying and weird sort of way, you see the Professor stood in the middle of her laboratory at SItU Headquarters. She seems to be about ten feet and a million miles away from you simultaneously.

"Professor! You got this Time Tornado working again!" You reply with glee.

"The wha..? Oh, I see. Yes, I told you I would," Professor Wylie replies with a triumphant grin. "It's taking massive amounts of energy to keep it open, Hills. Is the tornado wide enough your end for you to enter?"

"About three-and-a-half feet diameter, I'll have to stoop. But, Professor, there's..."

"Tell me in a minute, Hills," interrupts Professor Wylie. "You must enter the tornado now; I can't keep it open much longer. And be sure to duck, I don't want you to arrive home without your head!"

Without any further hesitation you run towards the tunnel of blue light, ducking at the last moment.

"Tally-ho!"

Turn to **021.**

053

As you ponder the purpose of the half-cricket ball nestled in the palm of your hand, you notice a laminated document affixed to the inside of the cabinet door. The document contains a series of clear diagrams and terse, bullet-point instructions. Atop the page is the title:

Safe Use of Archaeological Blasting Ordnance.

"Ooooh, bombs!" you coo.

Turn to **080.**

054

Feeling unsettled by the inhuman breathing sounds, and suspecting that some deadly danger might be lying in wait for you behind the nondescript door, you choose not to enter the Dorm but instead sneak quietly back to the junction to reconsider.

Will you now take the West Passage to investigate the Canteen and Kitchen? If so, turn to **186.**

Or will you press on Northwards to the Green Airlock for a better look through the porthole at what lies beyond it? To do this, turn to **036.**

055

You take a few deep breaths to sooth your nerves, and then look about yourself for an idea of what to do next.

The East Passageway, in which you currently stand, runs to quite a length and ends with a single windowless and formidable-looking Red Airlock.

A nimble sprint across the junction would see you in the West Passageway, which is quite short and ends at a steel-grey coloured single door marked simply as *Stores*.

If you were to go South, via the Green Airlock, you would find yourself heading back the way you originally came, and could quite quickly return to Orange Airlock where you first tumbled into this nightmare. Professor Wylie did tell you not to move from there, after all.

Do you want to head East down this corridor to the Sturdy Red Airlock? If so, turn to **006.**

Or would you rather dash across the junction and take the West Passage to investigate the Storeroom? To do this, turn to **099.**

Alternatively, you could scamper swiftly and silently South, and head to the relative safety of the Orange Airlock to await rescue by the Professor. You can tell her all about what's happening here when she regains contact. To take this course of action, turn to **031.**

056

In the silence of the Airlock the minutes seem to drag by, and you dare not move from the corner in which you crouch. Occasionally you hear the inhuman, electronic tones of the Chief Saturmek barking orders to its subordinates somewhere in the corridors beyond, each time it makes you jump a little, and each time the dreaded voice sounds closer than before. You stare at the hands on your watch; 10:47.

"Please hurry, Professor," you whisper to yourself. "If you don't come soon, they're bound to find me, and then..."

You dare not even finish the thought.

Turn to **052**.

057

You swing the door of the locker open to find that there's little of interest inside. You see a clean, fluffy bath towel and shower cap, and a few empty coat-hangers. You guess the Moonbase crew stored personal effects and fresh garments here while working outside.

You're about to close the door when you spy a small rectangular card on the floor of the locker, which you stoop to pick up. The item is roughly the same size as a credit card, and seems to be made of the same type of plastic. It has a hole punched in one corner and a metal ring threaded through it; it's probably meant to be worn on a lanyard, or perhaps it's a keyring. On one side bold, black text on a red background reads:

Moonbase Shackleton Health & Safety Andon Card.

The reverse side contains a body of smaller text, mostly bullet-pointed, providing clear and concisely-phrased reminders concerning the most important rules and regulations to observe when working in this area:

The Excavation Site on the Moon's surface can be accessed via the Grey Airlock Door. All personnel present must be fully dressed and equipped in an appropriate Pressure Suit before the Airlock is activated and opened.

Mechanical Excavation Equipment should always be housed in the hanger when not in use. It can only be operated by crew carrying the necessary activation license.

All monitoring consoles, system control consoles, and the Sterilisation Protocol Alpha One Self-Destruct Console are housed in the Site Manager's Cabin. These primary systems run in parallel to those housed in the Operations Centre.

The Interior Excavation Site is highly radioactive. Safe exposure time is limited to five hours.

Although it is believed the alien virus that killed the Original Occupants is extinct, extreme caution must be exercised when excavating and/or entering previously unexplored and/or uncatalogued areas of the Lunar Interior.

All Pressure Suits must be hung in the decontamination cabinet after use. They will be automatically cleaned, sterilised and decontaminated ready for next use.

On returning to the Moonbase, all personnel must remain in the decontamination chamber for four hours whilst Moonbase Systems monitor their health and welfare. Personnel should only enter other areas of Moonbase when given the all-clear.

A crib card of regulations for a new crewmember, presumably. Still, it was a handy find!

Now add 10 points to your Savvy Score and turn to **111**.

058

Examining the door of the Blasting Ordnance cabinet, you see a substantial, but traditional-looking keyhole.

"Some type of mechanical tumbler," you comment as you slip your hand into your pocket and produce the battered leather tri-fold wallet which contains your scientific tools. "Gotta be worth a try."

Now turn to **188**.

059

You can barely contain your joy at the thought of rescue, and feel that you're almost unshakeable faith in Professor Wylie is justified as you allow yourself a little whoop of delight and clap your hands. She knows where you are, she knows *when* you are, and rescue is just thirty minutes away... well, give-or-take a few minutes, knowing the Professor.

You glance at your wristwatch; it's a quarter past ten, or rather it was back at SItU Headquarters when you left, which means you'll be back in time for elevensies, when Mrs. Mallard brings round the tea trolley. But your exhilaration is suddenly tempered by thoughts of the poor spaceman outside, face down in the cold dust of the Lunar desert...

You have about thirty minutes to kill, so what do you think should you do?

Will you continue to stay put and wait, as Professor Wylie instructed? If you choose to do what you've been told, then turn to **048**.

Will you exit this Airlock via the North door and have a bit of a wander around Moonbase Shackleton, hoping to find someone in charge that you can tell about the crashed Moon-buggy... even though this might lead to awkward questions! If so, turn to **037**.

Or will you take matters into your own hands, climb into one of those orange Spacesuits and Moon-walk your way over the Lunar surface to the astronaut-in-distress? If this seems like the best idea, turn to **191**.

060

Do you feel that you should proceed with picking the cabinet's lock, hoping that the wires you glimpsed are nothing to worry about? To carry on lock-picking, turn to **193**.

Or do you think that the wires are part of an alarm system which could almost certainly alert the Saturmeks to your presence if tripped? Would you rather pack away your tools, leave the cabinet locked, and move on? If so, please turn to **175**.

061

Silently and swiftly, you retrace your footsteps, hurrying Southwards down the main passageway and towards the Green Airlock. Moments later you're through, and continue to head straight down the adjoining corridor.

A few hundred yards deftly and hurriedly covered sees you back where you first arrived on Moonbase Shackleton; the large Orange Airlock Door. With circumspect, you follow the simple three-step door-opening guide as before. The door swings outward, driven by entirely silent motors, and you step hastily into the small chamber. The Airlock door seals itself behind you, and you allow a quick glance through the porthole to ensure you weren't spotted or followed. Reassuringly, no Saturmeks are to be seen or heard in the vicinity.

"Hurry, Professor," you mutter as you turn your back on the door and crouch out of sight. "Please hurry... or Earth is finished!"

Now turn to **052**.

062

Eavesdropping on this private gathering of Saturmeks is no simple affair; short periods of silent study are frequently broken by an inhuman squawk from one, a *eureka* moment presumably, followed by all four talking at once!

You listen as best you can, and although most of what they discuss is far from clear, you certainly get the terrifying gist of their discoveries. This Ancient Stone Obelisk, it seems, is key. The Saturmeks reckon that if they take the artefact back into the Moon's interior, to the location where the Shackleton Team found it, they can somehow use it to crash the Moon into Earth!

As far as intelligence-gathering missions go, your findings are pretty sketchy, but you've learnt enough to know that you must do something to prevent this atrocity!

Now add 10 points to your Savvy Score and turn to **095.**

063

"Commander Rex King – Incident Log. Date is twenty-seventh of March, 2074. Base time is oh-six-thirty-seven hours. Unidentified craft sighted over the Moonbase. I repeat; type and origin of craft unconfirmed. Radar didn't pick it up, only sighted visually by chance from the canteen window by Lieutenant Lawson, who immediately reported to me. Last seen descending in the vicinity of Shackleton Crater, a little under a kilometre to the North."

The screen darkens momentarily then flickers back into life as a second entry plays.

"Base time is oh-six-forty-two hours. Have attempted to contact Earth Control, but our communications are being jammed. This alone could be construed as an act of aggression. With a crew of only eight currently manning Shackleton, I've opted to investigate the mystery craft myself. I'll take a buggy out to the landing site, which is less than a kilometre from here. Lawson is against the idea, but I've over-ridden her concerns. I'll be discrete... just in case."

The next entry plays. Commander King's worried face is encased in a space-helmet, and the backdrop is the inky blackness of the Lunar sky.

"I am within visual range of the craft. It's a saucer, quite small, possibly some sort of Scout Shuttle. Don't recognise the origin. I expect it's crewed by no more than four. I'm observing it from a discreet distance. No sign of activity. Unable to report back to Moonbase; communications still jammed."

"Saturmeks!" splutters King in his next entry, alarm evident in his trembling voice. "The Saucer hatch opened and four Saturmeks disembarked! Saturmeks, I swear! The situation's dire. I must get back to base."

You watch as the shaky point-of-view footage continues onscreen, King had forgotten to shut off the recorder in his panic. Breathing heavily, he clambers back into his buggy and accelerates off towards the base. You hear him panting, occasionally vocalising his fear and despair in a train of blurted, fractured phrases.

"Oh God, what can we do?! Saturmeks! Must warn Earth. If they take Moonbase... Lord, help us, we'd have to self-destruct!"

You continue to watch the ghastly point-of-view account as events unfold in real time on the little device in the palm of your hand. With the Moonbase in sight, a green energy bolt suddenly strikes the ground just ahead of the speeding buggy, silently throwing up a cloud of dust and vapour.

"No," screams King, his voice nearing hysterical. "They've spotted me!"

You watch the shaky footage as a second energy bolt strikes the front of the buggy and causes it to flip. King cries out, and then the recording falls all but silent save for the hiss of air escaping from a cracked helmet, and laboured breathing from the dying Commander. An indistinct and out-of-focus Lunar landscape is all that can be seen on the little screen now.

"Lieutenant Lawson, are you receiving? Lawson?!" You hear Commander King try his helmet communicator one last time between painful, oxygen-starved gasps. "Saturmeks, Lawson. Bloody Saturmeks! Hope you can hear this. Hope the jamming's dropped..."

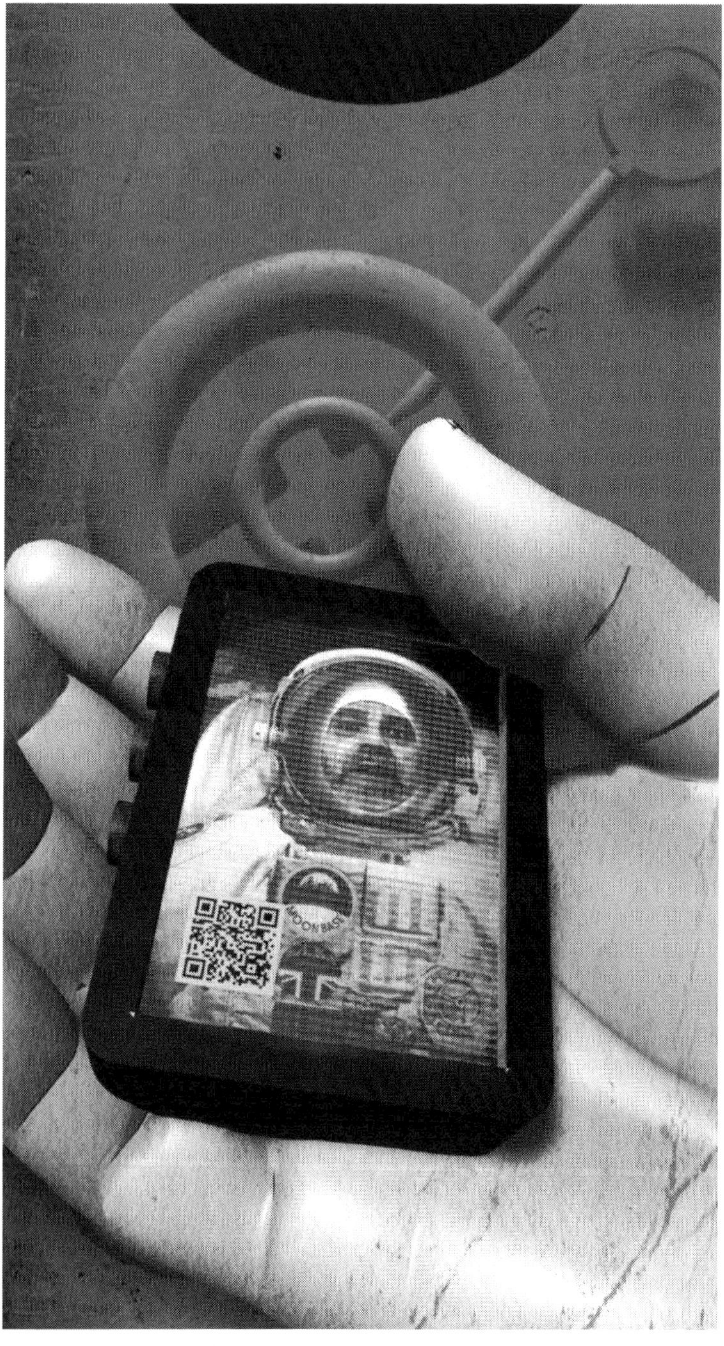

King words are punctuated by a series of violent, bloody-sounding coughs.

"Oh, Christ, I'm dying!" he mutters, with a voice now feeble and laboured. "Lawson, don't let the Saturmeks take the base. If the base falls, Earth falls. We must initiate Sterilisation Protocol Alpha One. Set the self-destruct timer and blow this place to kingdom-come, Saturmeks an' all. My Authorisation Code is 22401. It's up to you, Lawson. Do it. Do it!"

Be sure to *make a careful note of* Commander Rex King's Authorisation Code, as it seems of vital importance.

Now add 10 points to your Savvy Score, and turn to **197.**

064

Your hurried pace brings you back to the junction where the narrower East-West passage intersects with the main North-South corridor.

The Dormitory lies down the East corridor, and about twenty-five yards Northwards up the main corridor of you lies a Green Airlock-type door.

You desperately need an ally so decide to investigate the Dormitory in the hope of finding the eighth crew member still alive, but as you turn to head down the corridor a terrifying order is barked directly at you.

"Halt!" the electronic voice grates.

You turn to see a Saturmek gliding on its motivator ball up the corridor from the South Airlock area. The mechanical fiend's chest hatch opens, and the gun that extends from within the cavity is levelled directly at you.

064 - 065

"You are my prisoner. You will not move until ordered to do so. Obey, or die!"

Getting a better look at your captor now, you see that its metal casing is spattered liberally with dark red gouts of human blood.

"I presume you're the merciless brute that slaughtered the crew," you mutter.

Now turn to **015**.

065

The lengthy corridor which stretches out before you is as wide, featureless and purely utilitarian as the one you just left.

About fifty yards ahead of you, the corridor terminates with the white double doors marked *Operations Centre*. You hear a rhythmic two-toned *thum-thrum thum-thrum* sound coming from behind the Operations Centre doors, like an eerie mechanical heartbeat. The double doors have small porthole-style windows set into them at roughly head-height. From where you currently stand you can see a little of the Operations Centre through those windows, but are unable to make much out.

You also see that halfway down the corridor is a crossroads junction with secondary, smaller corridors leading off to the left and right.

Stooped like a thief on the prowl, you briskly tip-toe to the junction where a narrower East–West passage intersects the main corridor.

Moonbase Shackleton remains eerily silent, except for the unearthly *thum-thrum thum-thrum* of the Operations Centre, and perhaps the pounding of your own anxious heart, as you pause to look about.

Now turn to **073**.

066

Lawson manages a gentle smile of encouragement toward you.

"Got a cyber-chip in my head," she tells you. "Hacked into the Saturmek comms. Four Saturmeks on the base; a red commander, a scientist, and two thugs. They're all in the Operations Centre at the top of the North Corridor now. They think they've killed everyone, so their guard is down. Didn't reckon on us, eh?"

You brave a sympathetic smile and nod in agreement as Lawson's dying stare meets your eyes.

"Go back to the junction and head up through the Green North Airlock. Take the right passageway off the Main Corridor leading to the Red Airlock and enter the Decontamination Chamber. That chamber leads to the excavation site... and the Sterilisation Protocol Alpha One Self-Destruct Console. Enter... my code... then hit the button to... blow this place, us, and the Saturmeks to smithereens. I know... you're probably a bit... frightened, but it has to be done."

Lawson exhales a long, mechanically-assisted sigh as her eyes dullen and her head lolls limply to one side. The Dorm falls silent.

Lawson's dead, and Earth dies in just a few hours.

It's time to go!

Will you try to save the Earth by undertaking a suicide-mission to blow-up the base? If so then add 10 points to your Savvy Score and turn to **041.**

Or should you put all your faith in being rescued by Professor Wylie before time runs out, and hope she has a solution to the terrible peril Earth is in? To choose this option add 10 points to your Savvy Score and then turn to **013.**

067

You creep down the short passageway to the blue-framed door, but as you reach to open it, you still your hand in hesitation. What's that sound? Pressing your ear against the door you listen intently. There's a weird, irregular and laboured rasping coming from within the room; strangely mechanical, inhuman breathing sounds. The longer you listen, the more reluctant you are to find out what the cause is. Perhaps these strange rasping breaths are being made by some sort of clogged air conditioning unit? But then again, maybe a surviving crewmember is in there… wearing a Spacesuit? Or, worst-case scenario, could it be that there's a battle-damaged, malfunctioning Saturmek lurking in there?

Should you make a quick about-face and return to the junction? If so, turn to **054.**

Or have you set your mind on opening the door and entering the Dorm? To do this, turn to **088.**

068

Having detected that you've securely sealed the Airlock behind you, the chamber automatically pressurises and artificial Earth-normal gravity kicks in. A calm pre-recorded voice announces that it's now safe to disrobe. You promptly pop off the helmet and take a moment to enthusiastically rub your itchy nose with a gloved hand. Then you clamber out of the now-loose-fitting one-piece with ease.

You study the small box Commander King had been clutching. It appears to be plastic, about the size of a packet of twenty Silk Cut but with rounded corners, and mostly matt black but one of the wider surfaces is grey and has a glassy sheen to it. You see there are four small recessed buttons running down one side, labelled REC, FF, REV and PLAY. It must be some sort of cassette tape recorder, you reason, so you jab the PLAY button.

The grey screen illuminates as video playback begins. You immediately recognise the bushy-browed, unshaven face which appears, looking stern and a little perturbed, as that of the late Commander.

Turn to **063**.

069

Professor Wylie looks down to her bowl, picks up the spoon again and prods idly at the cooling suet.

"You know the Saturmeks, Hills," she says softly. "They're ruthless murderers, and you showed immense courage in both thought and deed when you went up against a squad of them alone."

"You did tell me to stay put," you add. "But I had to try, sorry."

"I did tell you to stay put, yes," replies the Professor, slowly looking up from her pudding to meet your eyes with a mischievous smile. "But... Earth threatened with utter destruction, a squad of Saturmeks running amok, the Moonbase crew dead or dying; and at great personal risk you took it upon yourself to save the World. That's my Hills!"

"It's good to be home safe, Professor," you smile.

"Relieved to have you home safe, Hilary," returns the Professor with a broad beam. "And it's also fascinating to learn that the Saturmeks are still at large out there in space. We had hoped the germ bombs devised back in '97 had finished them off for good, but always suspected that there might be a few survivors that escaped. It's a pity that current rocket technology doesn't allow us to take the fight to them, but at least it seems we have decades to prepare."

"I'm pretty certain there were no Saturmek survivors this time," you say.

"Not much chance of that, it seems," affirms Professor Wylie. "It was very resourceful of you to trigger a Moonquake to thwart their plan. There's something quite wonderfully *force majeure* about your solution, don't you think? Well done, Hills. I'm very proud of you and, I must say, I couldn't have done better myself."

"Professor Wylie…" interrupts a familiar voice. You both look over to see Captain Knight hurrying to your table.

"Top of the morning to you, Andy," greets the Professor. "Well, what demands is Sir Clive about to make on my precious time now?"

"He asks that you join him at Twycross Zoo immediately," replies Knight.

"Oh, yes? Up to some monkey business, is he?"

"That might be closer to the truth than you think," explains Captain Knight. "Apparently one of the chimps there got hold of a marker pen last night, and this morning its keepers got in to find some very complex-looking mathematical formulae written on the walls of its enclosure."

"Well, I suppose I'd better pay this prestigious primate a visit," announces Professor Wylie as she rises from the table. "Coming, Hills?"

You jump to your feet, raring to go.

"Ditch the spacesuit, and bring a banana or two, Hills," calls back the Professor as she breezes out of the room.

"Never a dull moment," you quip to Captain Knight, and then you chase after the Professor on your way to a new adventure.

The End.

070

Going it alone against a squad of Saturmeks, you decide, would be a suicide mission. You'd be mad to step out of this Airlock and into a Moonbase that's potentially crawling with those murderous alien machines; you'd get yourself killed in a minute! Then Professor Wylie would come along, not knowing what she was getting herself into, find you missing, go looking for you and end up dead as well!

No, you can't have that. Besides, the Professor had clearly instructed; "Wherever you end up, stay put! Don't wander off!"

You wonder how long you'll actually have to wait before Professor Wylie manages to come to the rescue. However long it takes, it's going to seem like a lifetime! But you know the smartest thing to do is stay put and stay quiet. When the Professor does make contact, you're sure she'll know exactly what to do.

Until then, discretion, in this case, is most definitely the better part of valour.

Now turn to **056.**

071

You know when you're up really high and there's very little to stand on? Or perhaps you're hanging from a precipitous ledge by just your fingertips? As your stomach turns somersaults and your legs become lead, someone will unfailingly offer the sagely advice of *don't look down*. It's now that you find yourself experiencing that same stomach-churning, *I'm gonna fall* sensation as you take in the vastness of the dull grey vista and the endless, all-consuming pitch-dark sky.

"Don't look up," you mutter to yourself.

Focused on the welfare of the prone figure a few hundred yards ahead, you force yourself to shut all other thoughts and considerations out of your mind; you know if you stop to question your actions now, or pause to take stock of the situation you find yourself in, you're likely to freak out.

Having now gotten a grip, you find yourself bounding across the Lunar surface with relative ease and a resolute purpose. The suit you wear is designed to be a short-term fix for those fleeing disaster, and thankfully by necessity it's considerably more flexible and substantially less bulky than other pressure suits you've seen in use since joining SItU. You're running on the Moon!

You skid to a dusty halt as you reach the motionless spaceman. He's lying some distance from the overturned Moon-buggy, which has stopped spewing gas but is still spurting showers of sparks every few seconds. He's lying face-down, frozen in a crawling posture, his gauntleted right hand clawing at the rocky surface, his left hidden beneath his torso, and his sprawled legs locked mid-kick. This doesn't look promising. You crouch beside him, take a firm grasp on his right shoulder, finding to your dismay

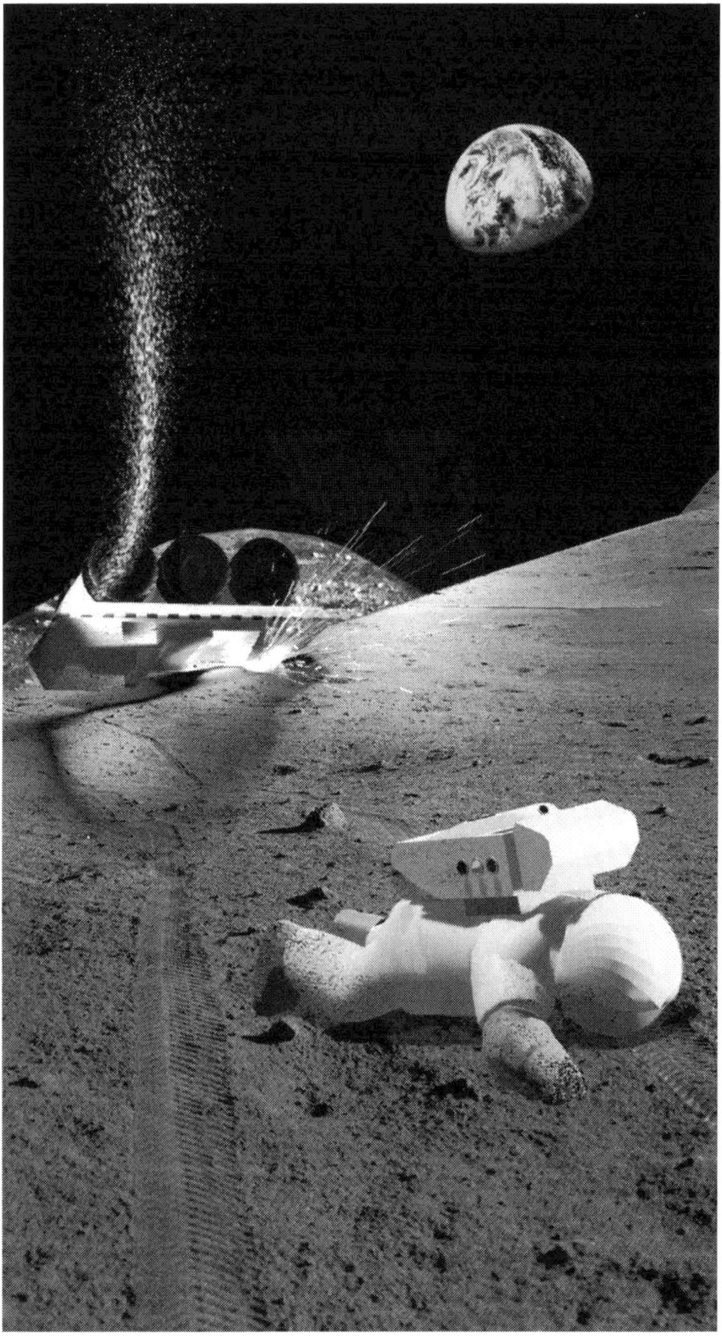

that the pressure suit is quite saggy around his body, and flip him over onto his back.

The face behind the cracked visor is of an older man, all grey bushy eyebrows, salt-and-pepper stubble and deep crow's feet. The dark blood around his nostrils glisten with ice crystals, his swollen tongue protrudes from between cyanosis lips, and his bulging eyes fix you with the glassy, unblinking stare of the dead. According to the suit-patch on his chest, his name was King and he was the Commander of Moonbase Shackleton.

You've seen death before but, still, you allow a heavy sigh of lament to escape.

Then you notice something clutched in Commander King's left hand, clasped to his chest as if it was of great importance and needed protecting. You prise open King's fingers and retrieve a grey and black plastic box about the size of a packet of cigarettes. You'll take it back to the Moonbase immediately because there's nothing else you can do for this poor man.

Now turn to **097.**

072

The West Passageway, leading off to your left, is quite short and ends with simple and homely-looking, wood-effect double-doors. A sign above the doors reads *Canteen and Kitchen*. Although the doors contain sizeable Perspex windows, no lights are on in the room beyond; all is in darkness.

The East Passageway, which leads off to your right, is somewhat longer and ends with a single windowless door. This door would be almost indistinguishable from the wall it's set in, if not for the dark blue doorframe surround. Upon the door is fixed a hand-made sign which reads *Dorm – Knock and Enter* in fastidious marker pen.

About twenty-five yards ahead of you lies another Airlock-type door, this one is painted green. From where you stand you can see through its porthole that this well-lit Central Corridor continues.

Will you now:

Take the West Passage to investigate the Canteen and Kitchen? If so, turn to **186.**

Head down the East Corridor to see what the Dormitory has to offer? To do this, turn to **067.**

Press on Northwards to the Green Airlock for a better look through the porthole at what lies beyond it? If this is your choice, turn to **036.**

Or if you feel, perhaps, that you're heading in to mortal danger, and think it might be wiser to return to the Orange South Airlock and await rescue, then you should turn to **078.**

073

The West Passageway, which leads off to your left, is quite short and ends at a steel-grey coloured single door marked simply as *Stores*.

The East-leading Passage, to your right, is somewhat longer and ends with a windowless and formidable-looking Red Airlock Door.

About twenty-five yards ahead of you lies the white, double doors marked *Operations Centre*; the source of the weird electronic heart-beat.

Will you now:

Take the West Passage to investigate the Storeroom? If so, turn to **028**.

Head down the East Corridor to the Sturdy Red Airlock Door? To do this, go to **006**.

Press on Northwards to the Operations Centre and dare to peek through the portholes to find out what's happening in this important-sounding room? To choose this action, turn to **089**.

074

The locking wheel spins effortlessly through several full turns, and then the Green Airlock door swings gracefully inwards. You step cautiously through into the Operations Area of the Moonbase, being sure to leave the door as you found it.

Now turn to **065**.

075

Your conscience can't allow you to leave that poor man out there if there's a chance that he's still alive and, given the apparent urgency of the situation, you feel that running up and down corridors looking for someone to help would just waste vital minutes. You take a look at the Spacesuits, neatly arranged on their coat hooks. They all look identical; the same generic size, shape and cut. *"One size, fits no one"*, as SItU's Quartermaster might quip. You've never worn a Spacesuit before, but have seen several in use over the past few months, and how difficult can putting one on be?

Suddenly your train of thought is rudely and quite alarmingly interrupted as, in the middle of the room, a shimmering ball light appears accompanied by a worryingly familiar ethereal crackle of raw, angry energy. No bigger than a tennis ball, the ghostly orb looks to be spinning at an incredible velocity as it phases through umpteen shades of blue. The mysterious sphere suddenly swells to the size of a football, and then morphs rapidly into something more conical in shape, still spinning wildly it now disturbingly resembles a tornado. Pressing yourself into a corner, you keep as much distance between you and the phantasmal whirling dervish as you can, but the fearsome, tapering column of electric-blue light creeps inch-by-inch toward you – as if it's seeking you out in a game of blind-man's bluff – and then topples. Extremely unnerved and daring not to move a muscle, you're now staring into the wide maw of a sideways tornado of swirling, spinning plasma and lightning!

A crackling, echoing voice, faint and barely distinct, whispers from deep within the ethereal funnel...

"Hilary Hills? Can you hear me, Hilary? It's Professor Wylie."

"Professor!" You call back, feeling your spirits soar. "I can hear you... just about."

"I've got the Berwyn Device working, and it's located you! I managed to combine the Temporal Condenser Circuit with the Tachyon Capacitor to create a Fugacious Spatial Vortex from me to you. That's what you're looking at now, and how I'm able talk to you. I know where you are, Hills, and I can bring you home!"

"How do I get back, Professor? Is this tornado-thing the *Phew-gaseous Special Vortex?*"

"Yes, but I need to make the passage considerably bigger so you can enter it. It shouldn't take me too long. Half an hour should do it. Hold tight, Hills, just stay exactly where you are."

"But, Professor, there's..."

The funnel of blue swirling light crackles, judders, then suddenly it distorts into a doughnut shape.

"Oh crikey!" You hear the Professor exclaim as the Fugacious Spatial Vortex turns a dark purple in hue before blinking out of existence.

And then, as before, you stand alone in the silence of the airlock. Half an hour, Professor Wylie had promised, that's all, and then you're out of this nightmare. Time enough, you decide, to go to the rescue of that poor soul outside!

You turn your attention back to the Spacesuits, and take one down from its hook. To your quiet delight you discover that it was obscuring an instructional document affixed to the wall behind it. The poster is headlined:

The Windak Emergency Evacuation Pressure Suit.

Instructions for Use.

You scan the tutorial, paying more attention to the diagrams than text, and get the gist of it. The suit is designed to be slipped on in just moments; it seals itself airtight and adjusts to the wearer's figure. The helmet self-locks to the neck seal. It's designed for emergency use only; if the Moonbase needs to be evacuated, and should any Crew members find themselves unable to reach their own bespoke Spacesuits, they can survive outside wearing one of these... for a while. You mark that battery life and air supply limited to approximately three hours.

"Basically, it's a space-age life jacket," you summarise to yourself as you clamber into your chosen suit and zip it up from crotch-to-chin.

The helmet, which you grab from beneath the bench, is of a classic goldfish bowl design. As you slip it over your head, the neck-seal of your suit reaches up to meet it with an unnerving suction sound. Then, with a satisfying gulp-clunk, the transparent globe is firmly secured. You hear a short series of whirs and clicks issue from inside the suit as the automatic life support systems activate.

You head to the Airlock Door and look for a means of opening it. Being an emergency exit, the operating procedure is swift and simple; a chunky, rubber-coated handle in the middle of the door is set on lock, a curved arrow indicates you turn the handle ninety degrees anti-clockwise to depressurise the chamber and unlock the door. Without hesitation you grasp the handle and give it a hearty twist. From an unseen speaker somewhere in the chamber, a pre-recorded female voice announces in calm tones that emergency decompression has commenced. You feel a gust of air tug at the fabric of your suit as the voice begins to count down the seconds from fifteen, and then the suit inflates and stiffens about your body in response to the venting atmosphere. The room falls profoundly silent before the recorded countdown gets to three.

"Two... one..." You count to yourself.

The Orange Airlock Door swings noiselessly outward, causing a small eddy of surface dust to rise and curl like smoke.

"One-sixth Earth gravity from here on in, Hills," you remind yourself as you step over the threshold and firmly plant your foot on silvery-grey ground. "Mind the gap!"

Add 10 points to your Savvy Score.

Now turn to **071.**

076

You feel adrenaline kick in. Your heart's pounding in your chest and your blood runs cold. The spaceman outside is dead; killed by the Saturmeks. They've also murdered the remaining crew; they're lying around dead somewhere on the Moonbase! You're here all alone.

"Get a grip, Hilary Hills!" You scald in sotto.

The Saturmeks don't know about you, and perhaps they need not find out if you can keep your head down and stay quiet.

Thirty minutes, Professor Wylie had promised, that's all, and then you're out of this nightmare. But the Red Saturmek spoke about the destruction of Earth! You can't just sit around and let them get on with it, can you?! You ask yourself, what would the Professor do? Well, she'd wade in and do everything she could to stop the Saturmeks, of course. Then you ask; what would the Professor expect of you?

Should you stay put, keep down and keep quiet until Professor Wylie comes to your rescue? Perhaps you can fill her in on what's happening in about half an hour. If you think this is the best thing to do, turn to **070.**

Or should you take a swift and furtive recce around the Moonbase to learn what more you can of the Saturmek plan to destroy Earth? If you chose to do this, turn to **176.**

077

"Yeah, it's best you keep hidden until rescue gets here," agrees Lawson. "Nothing you can do against Saturmeks on your own. You can fill the Marines in on the facts when they arrive."

You nod in agreement, not wishing to correct Lawson's false assumption. There are no burly Marines coming, and your best hope is a slightly eccentric, slightly-built genius who's currently tinkering with weird technology back in the year 1974!

"Got a cyber-chip in my head," continues Lawson between gasps of pain. "Hacked into the Saturmek comms. Four Saturmeks on the base; a red leader, a scientist, and two thugs. They're now all in the Operations Centre at the top of the North Corridor. They think they've killed everyone, so their guard is down. Didn't reckon on us, eh?"

You brave a sympathetic smile as Lawson's dying stare meets your eyes.

"Go back to the junction and head down to the South Airlock. Hide in there. There's also Emergency Evac Suits if you need to exit the base in a hurry."

"Come with me," you urge. "We can hide together."

Lawson exhales a long, mechanically-assisted sigh as her head lolls limply to one side. Then the dorm falls deathly silent.

Lawson's dead.

It's time to go.

Add 10 points to your Savvy Score and turn to **013.**

078

Moments later you're back where you first arrived on Moonbase Shackleton; the large Orange Airlock Door. With circumspect, you follow the simple three-step door-opening guide as before.

The door swings outward, driven by silent motors, and you step hastily into the small chamber.

The Airlock door seals itself behind you, and you allow a quick glance through the porthole to ensure you weren't spotted or followed. Reassuringly, no Saturmeks are to be seen or heard in the vicinity.

"Hurry, Professor," you mutter as you turn your back on the door and crouch out of sight. "I'm not ready to die!"

Now turn to **052**.

079

Sir Clive returns to his desk, seats himself before you like a residing judge, and takes a few agonisingly long and silent moments to consider your reply.

"Is there anything in what Hills is saying, Vyvian?"

Professor Wylie shoots you a sideways glance and offers a brief smile of encouragement.

"I don't doubt it, Sir Clive," she states, choosing her words carefully. "Hilary Hill's conduct was indeed very out of character on this occasion, but being sucked bodily into a space-time vortex without any sort of protective shielding must be an immense physical and psychological assault, the likes of which no human has ever experienced.

I suspect that Hills arrived at Moonbase Shackleton in a shocked frame of mind; disassociated, and probably in a fugue state. To be honest, I'm surprised the experience wasn't fatal, or at the very least permanently damaging to Hill's psyche."

Sir Clive turns his attention back to you.

"And how are you feeling now, Hills?" he asks, quite gruffly. "Any signs of permanent damage from your ordeal – mind, body or soul – do you think?"

"When I was up there, in the future, it felt like some weird waking dream, Sir Clive," you explain as best you can. "Like it wasn't actually real – or really actual – and I was simply an observer... even to the point of feeling like I was just observing myself and my own actions in some bizarre way. Like... I was... fiction."

"Disassociation, see?" adds the Professor helpfully.

"But now," you continue, "it's feels like I've just woken up. Everything's as usual. I feel perfectly normal, actually actual, and wonderfully ordinary again. Just my typical everyday self!"

"Good for you, Hilary," Professor Wylie says and shoots you another cheerful glance.

"So, Hills," begins Browne as he arches his back and squares his shoulders. "To your credit we now know that the Saturmeks are still at large out there in space. We had hoped the germ bombs devised back in '97 had finished them off for good, but always suspected that there might be a few survivors that escaped. It's a pity that current rocket technology doesn't allow us to take the fight to them, but at least it seems we have decades to prepare."

Sir Clive pauses and takes his time to look you up and down, as if even now he's considering his verdict. Cowardice, he had said, and you wonder if he still holds that opinion of you.

"To your detriment, however, you failed to take any meaningful action against a present and obvious enemy when the opportunity presented itself. This dereliction of duty was, I believe, very much out of keeping with your usual character, and was the result of... well, I suppose from Vyvian's observations, we could call it shell-shock."

"Oh, shell-shock! A brilliant turn-of-phrase, Sir Clive, you obviously have an excellent grasp of the ins-and-outs of the human mind," affirms the Professor.

She's buttering him up, you think. Good ol' Wylie really is on my side, thank goodness.

"Yes, rather," replies Browne, sounding rather pleased with himself. "So, Hills, I deem that you will not be held culpable for your inaction against enemy forces. Professor Wylie thinks that the balance of your mind was disturbed, and I trust her counsel."

"Thank you, Sir Clive," you gasp with relief.

"However," Browne is quick to reply, an index finger raised for emphasis. "It's clear to me that you are in need rest and recuperation, so I'm placing you on a fortnight's paid leave effective immediately."

"I need help cleaning up the mess in my lab," interrupts the Professor.

"A fortnight's paid leave effective tomorrow," corrects Sir Clive. "During that time, you will liaise with our own Doctor Gardner for a routine psychiatric assessment. Thank you, Vyvian, Hills, that will be all."

And with his edict delivered, Sir Clive dismisses you both with a gesture of his hand and turns his attention back to his pile of paperwork.

Turn to **038**.

080

You skim-read the wordy text and glance over the helpful diagrams, garnering only the most essential information. The hemispheres, you learn, are powerful explosives, usually used by the military, but being employed here by the Moonbase Team in their excavations of the Moon's interior. The mines are analogue, clockwork basically, so they can't be disabled by an EMP attack.

Operating the mine is simplicity itself; peel off the backing paper, stick the mine to the desired obstruction, twist the little nipple-like dial atop the dome to set detonation at the desired time, press it to begin the countdown, and then retreat to a safe distance. Exactly what should be considered a safe distance is probably explained somewhere in the several thousand words of small print, but you don't have the time for trivial details and so decide the directive to retreat to a safe distance should be read as; *run like blazes!*

Being military ordinance, there's also a secondary method of detonation; the booby trap. Set in the side of the mine is a small ring-pull tab which, when tugged, detaches from the mine and pays out a several yards of fine trip wire. You stick the mine where you need it, and once the wire is payed out to the desired length and anchored to a suitable point, you press the tit to lock the wire and prime the mine. Then run like blazes because the next person to touch that wire goes *boom!*

Each mine, you notice, has a serial number etched on it. The first mine is marked 2112, the second is 2114. Be sure to *make a careful note of* these serials.

Now turn to **091.**

081

Just six feet of open space lie between you and the East Corridor; if you dare to make a dash for it, you'll be out of the Saturmek's gun-sights for a few vital moments. This should buy you enough time, you reckon, to dart to the room at the end of that corridor, barge in, and somehow secure the door.

You break into your sprint, covering five feet in a split-second, but then you hear the *vizzzz* of a Saturmek gun discharging and pain courses through your every nerve-ending. You crumple to the floor.

Your last thoughts are of Professor Wylie; you're afraid she'll suffer the same grisly fate as you when she finally manages to reach Moonbase Shackleton meaning to rescue you.

Then all is darkness and silence as you, Hilary Hills, out of place and out of time, die on the Moon in the year 2074AD.

The End.

082

A short and furtive walk sees you returning to the intersection. You glance around while considering your options. You could investigate a hitherto unexplored area of Moonbase Shackleton, or perhaps double-check on a previously-visited area again.

The East-leading passage, to your right, is rather long and ends with a windowless and formidable-looking Red Airlock Door.

About twenty-five yards ahead of you lies the white double doors marked Operations Centre; beyond which is the source of the ominous electronic heart-beat sound.

If you were to head South, via the Green Airlock, you would find yourself retracing your steps the way you originally came, and could quite quickly return to Orange Airlock where you first tumbled into this nightmare. Professor Wylie did tell you not to move from there, after all.

Will you now press on Northwards to the Operations Centre and dare to peek through the portholes to find out what's happening in this important-sounding room? To do this, turn to **089**.

Should you head down the East corridor to see what lies beyond that Red Airlock? If so, turn to **006.**

Or will you scamper swiftly and silently back to the South end of Shackleton and head to the relative safety of the Orange Airlock to await rescue by the Professor? You can tell her all about what's happening here when she regains contact. If you consider this the best action to take, then turn to **031**.

083

You watch as the Saturmeks scuttle across to a control console on the North side of the room. Realising this is your best chance to sneak out, you commit to making your getaway.

Again crawling on your hands and knees, you scurry the short distance back to the double doors and slip deftly through, unnoticed by the preoccupied Saturmeks. Once in the corridor you remain crouched as you hurry back to the junction, and take a sharp left to hide around the corner of the East Corridor.

You allow yourself a few moments to calm your nerves, chew a stick of spearmint gum, and consider your next move.

You study the communicator that you snatched from the Operations Centre. It looks like a miniaturised, futuristic walkie-talkie and seems pretty straight-forward enough to operate. You turn it on and thumb the *Call* button.

"Mayday. Mayday!" you hiss into the microphone, trying to shout quietly. "Can anyone hear me? Mayday!"

"This is Lovelock Orbital Beacon receiving," comes an immediate reply. "Go ahead, Mayday."

You fumble with the volume control, turning it down considerably while hoping Lovelock Orbital Beacon's unexpectedly quick response did not carry as far as the Operations Centre.

"This is Moonbase Shackleton," you report, speaking as clearly as you can and as loudly as you dare. "We've been attacked by Saturmeks. The crew are dead. Moonbase is now occupied by an extremely hostile Saturmek force."

"Did you say Saturmeks, Shackleton?!" The Operator at Lovelock can't hide the incredulity in his voice.

"Yes. Er, Affirmative, Lovelock. Saturmeks. Saturmeks!" you reply emphatically. "And they plan to destroy Earth! Send help. They must be stopped!"

"Message received and understood, Shackleton," replies Lovelock Beacon earnestly. "Will relay your information to the authorities immediately. Stand by... and Godspeed. Lovelock out."

You pocket the small communicator and hope your brief message was enough. Now, it's time to make your next move.

Add 10 points to your Savvy Score and turn to **055**.

084

You step gingerly into Dormitory, poised to flee at the first sign of any trouble, but as your eyes dart anxiously about the room you see no immediate danger.

The Dormitory is a large, rectangular room as sparse and impersonal as any MOD barracks you've seen. You count eight bunks, neatly-ordered and evenly spaced. Beside each bunk is a small chest of drawers, a few personal effects atop each one is the only indication that people call this place home; a pot of plastic flowers, framed photos, a cuddly toy mascot, a few books and magazines.

You see a door in the West wall which leads through to the shower-room and toilets. Another door in the South wall is marked as the Laundry Room. It's all functional and corporate, not at all jolly, you note with disdain.

The laboured, mechanical breathing sound continues uninterrupted by your intrusion. Cocking an ear, you determine that it's coming from a bunk in the far corner. You dare take a few paces closer and are alarmed to see a human figure awkwardly hiding in the cramped space beneath the bunk. A pair of eyes peer plaintively toward you from out of the gloom, and then a woman begins to crawl laboriously from the hiding place. You hurry over and stoop to assist her from out of the makeshift refuge, but despite your support she barely manages to rise to her feet before keeling backwards onto her bed. The woman, about twenty years your senior and dressed for sleep in silk pyjamas, is evidently in the most terrible agony; breathing through clenched teeth, her eyes now shut tightly. Embroidered on the breast pocket is her name; Claire Lawson.

"Claire," you gently utter. "Can you hear me, Claire?"

Lawson's eyes flicker open as she gasps, and she slowly, painfully, turns her head to face you.

"Rescue party? So soon?" She gasps, clearly fighting back near-unbearable pain. "Good. Was afraid my mayday call didn't transmit. You bring Marines? I asked for Marines."

"I'm here to help," you reply tactfully.

"Well beyond help, me," labours Lawson. "Saturmeks are here."

"They did this to you?" you ask, and you realise it's a needless question as it leaves your lips.

"Was coming off Night Shift," Lawson mutters in staccato bursts between laboured gasps. "Spotted a smallish craft glide over us as I ate supper. Reported it to Rex, and he went to investigate. Thought it was probably just wayward

Supply Drone, so I came to bed. Got woken up by a commotion down the hallway some short time later. Canteen... saw a Saturmek... a bloody Saturmek... slaughtering the Breakfast Club. I ran. Got hit. Left for dead. Crawled back here."

Now turn to **012**.

085

Professor Wylie looks down to her bowl, picks up the spoon again and prods idly at the cooling suet.

"You know the Saturmeks, Hills," she says softly. "They're ruthless murderers, and you wouldn't have stood much of a chance if you had gone up against a squad of them alone."

"You did tell me to stay put," you add.

"I did, yes," replies the Professor as she slowly looks up from her pudding and meets your eyes. "But I didn't know that Earth was threatened with utter destruction by a squad of Saturmeks running amok, or that the Moonbase crew were being slaughtered. It's true that you might not have made it back if you had decided to interfere further, but..."

"But what, Professor?" You ask, finding hard to hide the dismay in your voice.

"SItU was established, not only to investigate, but to *defend* Earth from uncanny threats, Hills, at any cost. *Any cost*. It is, after all, a branch of the Ministry of Defence, and sometimes operatives don't return. You know that."

The Professor's words are spoken softly, not in anger, and there's something in her manner which conveys that she's deeply disappointed in you. You stare down into your half-empty mug and feel utterly crestfallen.

"I have to make a report, Hills," Professor Wylie says with a sigh as she rubs her tired eyes. "I think you should stay here, get yourself another cuppa, and rest a while."

The Professor rises from the table and walks slowly towards the canteen exit, her hands thrust in her lab-coat pockets and her head bowed as if in deep contemplation.

You sit in silent self reflection, oblivious to the hubbub of the NAAFI's breakfasting patrons, feeling utterly alone.

Now turn to **192**.

086

You pace up and down the Airlock's length impatiently, your conscience pricking you at the thought of the injured astronaut, but Professor Wylie had insisted that you were to stay put wherever you ended up so that she could find you.

So here you are then; in an Airlock, on a Moonbase, in goodness-only-knows-what-year in the future, wondering when... if... Professor Wylie will ever be able to actually rescue you. Then your feelings of guilt double, and you immediately chastise yourself for doubting the Professor; she *will* keep her promise, and she *will* find you... any time now. When she arrives, you can tell her about the crashed Moon-buggy and she can take charge of the matter.

Suddenly, in the middle of the room, a shimmering ball of light appears accompanied by a worryingly familiar ethereal crackle of raw, angry energy. No bigger than a tennis ball, the ghostly orb looks to be spinning at an incredible velocity as it phases through umpteen shades of blue. The mysterious sphere suddenly swells to the size of a football, and then morphs rapidly into something more conical in shape, still spinning wildly it now disturbingly resembles a tornado. Pressing yourself into a corner, you keep as much distance between you and the phantasmal whirling dervish as you can, but the fearsome, tapering column of electric-blue light creeps inch-by-inch toward you – as if it's seeking you out in a game of blind-man's bluff – and then it topples. Extremely unnerved, and daring not to move a muscle, you're now staring into the wide maw of a horizontal tornado of swirling, spinning plasma and lightning!

A crackling, echoing voice, faint and barely distinct, whispers from deep within the ethereal funnel...

"Hilary Hills? Can you hear me, Hills? It's Professor Wylie."

"Professor!" You call back, feeling your spirits soar. "I can hear you... just about."

"I've got the Berwyn Device working, and it's located you! I managed to combine the Temporal Condenser Circuit with the Tachyon Capacitor to create a Fugacious Spatial Vortex from me to you. That's what you're looking at now, and how I'm able talk to you. I know where you are, Hills, and I can bring you home!"

"How do I get back, Professor? Is this tornado-thing the *Phew-gaseous Special Vortex?*"

"Yes, but I need to make the passageway considerably bigger so you can enter it. It shouldn't take me too long. Half an hour should do it. Hold tight, Hills, just stay exactly where you are."

"But, Professor, there's…"

The funnel of swirling blue light crackles and judders, then suddenly it distorts into a doughnut shape.

"Drat it!" You hear Professor Wylie curse as the Vortex darkens to purple before blinking out of existence.

Turn to **059**.

087

Lights detect your presence and flicker into life, showing you a Storeroom which is large, well-lit and well ordered. It's constructed from steel plate; the walls, floor and ceiling are bare metal, with visible welding seams and hefty rivets. Along each wall are rows of shelving units, each tidily loaded with provisions and equipment.

The contents of the shelving are mostly scientific-looking items at one end; circuit-boards, things that might be hand-held computers, equipment with lenses which are possibly telescopes or microscopes, perplexing technology of the future you can't possibly hope to recognise.

Against another wall are shelving units full of food-stuffs; a supermarket in miniature. You can see protein packs, bags of grains, cereals and rice, a sack of teabags, shrink-wrapped dried cured meats, plastic tubs of fruits in syrup, and many sundry other items. A large plastic keg, holding what you guess to be hundreds of gallons of water, sits on a sturdy tripod. The plumbing work that leads to and from it suggest that this is a water recycling machine. You're not thirsty, and most definitely lack any appetite right now.

Another tall, neatly-ordered bookcase-like unit contains paraphernalia you'd associate with construction or, more likely, archaeology; drills, picks, torches, sealable plastic tubs, battery-packs, light-poles... but, you note forlornly, nothing that could possibly be used as a weapon against Saturmeks. You take a snazzy-looking pen-light torch, test it and find the light it throws quite brilliant... Professor Wylie loves gadgets like this. You allow yourself a smile at the thought of getting home safe and making a gift of it to her.

But your moment of brief delight is cut cruelly short as an inhuman electronic bark cuts you to the bone.

"Halt!"

Now turn to **096**.

088

"I'll take just a quick peek," you whisper to yourself. "It might be someone in need of help."

You take one last quick glance about, making sure your escape route is clear should this prove to be the worst-case scenario, and push open the door.

Now turn to **084**.

089

Stooping low, sneaking quickly and silently, you reach the white double doors of the Operations Centre. Crouching below the porthole window of the left door, you listen intently. You hear the terrifyingly familiar electronic grate of indistinct Saturmek voices above the ambient rhythmic two-toned *thum-thrum thum-thrum* of the room.

You rise a little from your stoop to dare a quick peek through the thick glass of the porthole, and see that the Operations Centre itself is a glass geodesic dome.

Around the circumference of the room are a baffling array of command consoles, monitor screens, and all that usual mission-control jazz.

In the centre of the room four Saturmeks, two Drones, a Blue-domed Scientist, and their Red Commander, are gathered around a sandy-coloured stone monolith, which resembles a six-foot-tall Cleopatra's Needle with weird inscriptions on each side.

Turn to **039.**

090

HELLO, MINODORA.

THE SEALS OF YOUR SUIT ARE SECURE WITH 100% INTEGRITY.

SUIT INTERNAL TEMPERATURE REGULATED TO 21°C (+/- 0.5)

SUIT FITTING WILL OPTIMISE DURING AIRLOCK ATMOSPHERIC DECOMPRESSION TO ENSURE MAXIMISED COMFORT AND EASE OF MOVEMENT.

BE AWARE: IN-SUIT AIR SUPPLY CURRENTLY AT 21%.

ESTIMATED TIME UNTIL REPLENISHMENT NECESSARY: 0.75 HOURS.

ENJOY YOUR EXTRA-ATMOSPHERIC EXPERIENCE.

As the text fades from your sight, you're somewhat perturbed by the news that your Spacesuit only has enough oxygen to last three-quarters of an hour, but then you decide that you won't let this be a problem. After all, you don't intend to dilly-dally!

You then catch yourself quietly whistling *I'm the Urban Spaceman*. Nerves, you expect.

Now add 10 points to your Savvy Score and turn to **029**.

091

You give the chamber a last glance and notice a useful-looking satchel on a lower shelf. You grab it and carefully stow the two mines in your new bag. You then gather up your tool kit and stuff the wallet back into your pocket.

It's time to slip quietly away, like a thief in the night, via the steel door.

Now add 10 points to your Savvy Score and turn to **082**.

092

Six feet of open space lie between you and the corridor. If you make it, you'll be out of the Saturmek's gun sights for a few precious moments; enough time, you reckon, to burst into the Dorm and somehow secure the door.

"It's a fight or flight situation, Hills," you mutter under your breath. "And this is one fight I can't hope to win."

Muscles relax, limbs loosen. You're ready. You break into your sprint, covering five feet in a split-second. "Gonna make it!"

You hear the *vizzzz!* of a Saturmek gun discharging, pain shoots through your entire body and you pitch heavily to the floor.

Your last thoughts are of Professor Wylie; you fear she'll suffer the same fate if she manages to reach the Moonbase meaning to rescue you.

Then all is darkness and silence.

Now turn to **017.**

093

A light immediately comes on inside the cabinet.

"Like opening a fridge!" you sigh with relief. "Well, that explains the wiring."

Turn to **002.**

094

Have you, during your exploration of Moonbase Shackleton, learnt of any valid Authorisation Codes that you can use to LOGIN?

If you have, you should now turn to **162**.

If you haven't yet, you must turn to **131**.

095

But what can you do? Think, Hilary, think!

Are you, by any chance, carrying any explosive Blasting Ordnance?

If you are, turn to **174**.

If you do not any such explosives on your person, then you must turn to **046**.

096

Trembling, you turn slowly to see a Saturmek in the doorway with its gun levelled directly at you.

"You will remain where you are!" it barks aggressively. "You will not move. You will not resist! Obey!"

You are quick to raise your hands, surrendering to the utter hopelessness of your situation.

Now turn to **023**.

097

There's less urgency in your step now, and all sense of exhilaration is lost to you as you wearily make your way back to the yawning Orange Airlock.

"Don't look up," you remind yourself. "And don't look back."

Turn to **068**.

MINO'S BOOKS
YOU MAY BORROW, BUT PLEASE RETURN

098

Your eyes then fall on a large metal cabinet in the far corner. It's the size of a wardrobe and fabricated from the same welded and riveted metal as the room itself. On the cabinet door, stencilled in an ominous shade of mustard, are the words:

Danger – Blasting Ordnance.

In smaller text beneath instructions read:

Cabinet to be kept locked and sealed at all times. If access is required seek authorised key-holder's permission.

"Bingo!" you chirp gleefully as you hurry across the room.

Turn to **058**.

099

You dash across the junction, thankfully unseen, and follow the West Passageway the short distance to the door marked *Stores*.

The door, you find, is made of steel – not lighter alloys or plastics like the others in the base – as is the wall into which it is embedded. It's secured with a simple sliding bolt, which moves with oiled ease. You cautiously enter the Storeroom.

Now turn to **087**.

100

"Long story," gasps Lawson through the pain. "You get the *Brodie's Notes* version. Come closer."

Lawson's chill grip tightens as she rasps a deep intake of breath. You lean in, waiting to hang on to every whispered word.

"Last year a wide, deep shaft was found in the Lunar surface. Precision cut. Engineered. A team went down. The shaft leads to the Moon's interior, and a sprawling network of corridors and chambers. We called it the Shackleton Well, because it's pretty close to the crater of that name."

Lawson pauses momentarily, and closes her eyes as her hand further tightens over yours. She's evidently fighting back a surge of pain. She licks her parched lips, loosens her clasp a little and continues, eyes still closed.

"You see, the Earth's Moon isn't natural. It's an immense spaceship, several millennia old, built and manned by an alien race of giants. We nicknamed 'em the *Nephilim*; it's a Bible thing, I'm told."

An involuntary gasp escapes you. You've often looked up into the night sky on a clear, cold night and stared at the Moon. Odd, how despite its allusions to *l'amour* in pop songs and romance flicks, you've always thought it looked sad and kinda creepy. For years, no matter how hard you tried, you couldn't see the *Man in the Moon*, until one night it just kind of clicked; and there he was for you to see. You remember the chill that ran down your spine that night, because, to you at least, the Man in the Moon looked to be screaming.

"They're still down there," utters Lawson. "The Nephilim dead are scattered throughout the inside of this Moon. Killed by a virus, the pathologists suggest."

"A disease?!" you blurt.

"Don't worry. Long-extinct... probably," adds Lawson. "The find was kept secret. Moonbase Shackleton was built quickly and covertly to study and excavate the interior. The Well entrance is just a couple of minutes East of here. The current crew were archaeologists... and a building engineer... cartographer... basically on care-taker duties. Military was planning to build something bigger and more permanent in the coming months."

"Why the military?" you ask.

"The technology down there is... well, those dead giants used to fly the Moon, so it's pretty damn impressive."

Lawson chuckles grimly, which clearly causes her further pain. It takes her a moment to recompose herself before she can continue.

"How the Saturmeks got to know about this top-secret project is anyone's guess," she adds. "But I s'pose they've got spies and agents on Earth, maybe."

"So, the Saturmeks want this Nephilim technology for themselves?" you speculate.

"No," hisses Lawson curled lips and gritted teeth. "The Saturmeks intend to decipher the alien technology, get the Moon's engines up an' running and then crash it into Earth! Revenge for that failed occupation of... uh... nearly two hundred years ago. Seems they can hold a grudge for a very long time! They can do it too... I've poked about inside their systems... damn, they're smart! They'll probably have it all figured it out in a few hours."

"We've got to stop them!" you gasp.

"Yep. And here's how," pants Lawson, now trembling as pain continues to wrack her dying body. "Sterilisation Protocol Alpha One! This base is mined to self-destruct. It's a protocol measure put in place to safeguard against a re-emergence of the virus, or something else dangerously alien coming up from the shaft. When we took this job, we knew there was a chance we might die up here, but we thought the danger would come from within the Moon… and if it did, we knew to protect Earth we'd have to atomise this area… this Moonbase, the Shackleton Well an' all."

Lawson makes a sharp intake of breath, arches her back, and then her grasp on your hand loosens considerably. Her strength is ebbing away.

"My Authorisation Code… you'll need it… *make a careful note of* this… my Authorisation Code is 30141592654."

"Blimey," you tactlessly murmur.

"Easy to remember. Easy as Pi… but a zero instead of a decimal point," reassures Lawson. "You want to stop the Saturmeks from destroying the entire Earth? Then use my Authorisation Code to set the Sterilisation Protocol Alpha One self-destruct."

"I've got to blow up the Moonbase?!" you gasp.

"You gotta end the Saturmeks before they end mankind!" hisses Lawson with grim resolve.

Now turn to **189.**

101

The passing minute feels like an eternity as the orange light continues to strobe and the klaxon wails on. You feel the spacesuit automatically adjust itself around your body as the chamber's atmosphere is voided.

DECOMPRESSING... 03

DECOMPRESSING... 02

DECOMPRESSING... 01

DECOMPRESSION COMPLETE.

The klaxon quietens in increments until silent and, as the orange beacon blinks out, the lighting returns to normal levels.

AIRLOCK DOOR OPENING.

You stand and watch the door swing gracefully, silently outwards on its huge hinges. Over the threshold lies the grey dust and glistening ice crystals of the barren Lunar surface.

You summon up your courage, steel your resolve, and then step through the yawning porthole into the desolate landscape.

Now turn to **167.**

102

Slowly, with increasing steadiness and confidence, you half-walk and half-bunny hop along the light-pole lined pathway to the main excavation area. As you near the illuminated chasm in the ground you begin to appreciate the scale and significance of it; a geometrically perfect circular hole, probably no less than forty feet in diameter, bored straight into the Lunar bedrock. Numerous tripod-mounted work lights are placed thither-and-yon, a few are switched on.

You approach with caution until you're just a few short steps from the edge of this gaping maw. Could this be a sink hole? An impact crater? An ancient magma vent? You side step to a nearby work light and flick the chunky on-switch. A football stadium-strength light suddenly floods the inner shaft and you see that it's lined with perfectly smooth and symmetrical tiles. Massive metal rungs are set into the wall, like those of a colossal ladder, and they run down the depth of the shaft and into the impenetrable darkness far, far below.

Now turn to **157**.

103

Are you, by any chance, carrying any explosive Blasting Ordnance?

If you are, turn to **153**.

If you don't have any such explosives on your person, then you must turn to **122**.

104

PLEASE BE AWARE: IN-SUIT AIR SUPPLY CURRENTLY AT 10%.

ESTIMATED TIME UNTIL REPLENISHMENT NECESSARY: 0.16 HOURS.

"That's about ten minutes!" you exclaim. "Where does the bloomin' time go?!"

You do some rough-an'-ready arithmetic in your head; the elevator ride down took five minutes… thereabouts… and it must be a three-minute walk – the way you shamble in a spacesuit – between the Well and the Airlock…

"I've got to get out of here!" you gasp.

You keep your breathing shallow and steady as you turn your back on the mysterious ancient alien pilot. You're reluctant to leave because you feel there's an answer down here, but you've got to get back to the Moonbase or you'll suffocate!

Now turn to **195**.

105

"No," you mutter to yourself. "Not this way. Not like this."

You hit the 'N' key and watch as the video screen and keyboard retract back into the cabinet. A fresh, new sheet of smoked glass forms over the top of the console, like watching ice form on the surface of a pond in a speeded-up film.

Exiting the cabin, mind racing and short on time, you look around again.

Now turn to **138**.

106

You hit the 'N' key. The screen replies immediately with a sombre message:

```
We are sorry to learn that a member of the
Command Team has been lost.

Please proceed by entering your Authorisation
Code.
```

You now have to type a valid Authorisation Code into the computer terminal.

You're going to perform a similar calculation to that done at the Red Airlock earlier, and here's how to do it:

Add all the individual digits of the code to give you a total. Now add 7 to that total to give you a new total. *

The New Total is the reference you should **now turn to.**

---

* For instance, if the code is 12345, then do the following sum: 1+2+3+4+5, which adds up to a total of 15. Then add 7, to give a new total of 22. In this example, you would now turn to 22.

107

You approach the garage and realise that there really is nothing more to it than first impressions led you to believe; three walls, a sloping roof and a few scaffold-pole support pillars. It really is little more than a shelter, built with all the architectural finesse of a cow shed.

Aside from the two-seater Moon-buggies, there are three industrial-looking trucks parked up, each is of the same robust basic tractor design, but each has its own unique attachment; an arm-and-shovel excavator, a bulldozer blade, and a large drill. You approach the bulldozer, just to satisfy a passing notion that it might make for a useful anti-Saturmek weapon, but immediately realise that an ignition card must be inserted into a slot to get the thing going. You're not going to manage hot-wiring something like this!

Dismissing the idea of trying to drive one of these Lunar vehicles, you look beyond the trucks, deeper into the *cow shed*.

Turn to **169.**

108

Then it all happens at once. A window shatters, a glowing purple-blue beam, like a bolt of ultra-violet lightning, flashes past your visor, missing your head by just inches, and a console behind you silently explodes.

Instinctively you duck, and a second bolt zips overhead, blowing out the rear cabin wall. You dare look up and see a Saturmek drone gliding at speed on its rollerball across the Lunar surface and towards the cabin, its illuminated eye-lens is flashing angrily, and you can imagine its furious ranting.

The situation is ludicrous; in about four seconds none of this will matter, so why cower from a Saturmek now? You rise to your feet and stare defiantly at the advancing mechanical fiend.

"Too late," you shout, unsure if it can hear you, but, by golly, it makes your final moments alive feel worthwhile. "Saturmeks loose! I win! Earth lives!"

The Saturmek fires again, and the bolt hits you squarely in the chest. Absolute agony tears through your every nerve and you feel your legs buckle under you. As you pitch forward, consciousness abandoning you, your eyes fall on the video screen and the new message that flashes upon it.

```
Sterilisation Protocol Alpha One... ABORTED.
```

Now turn to **128.**

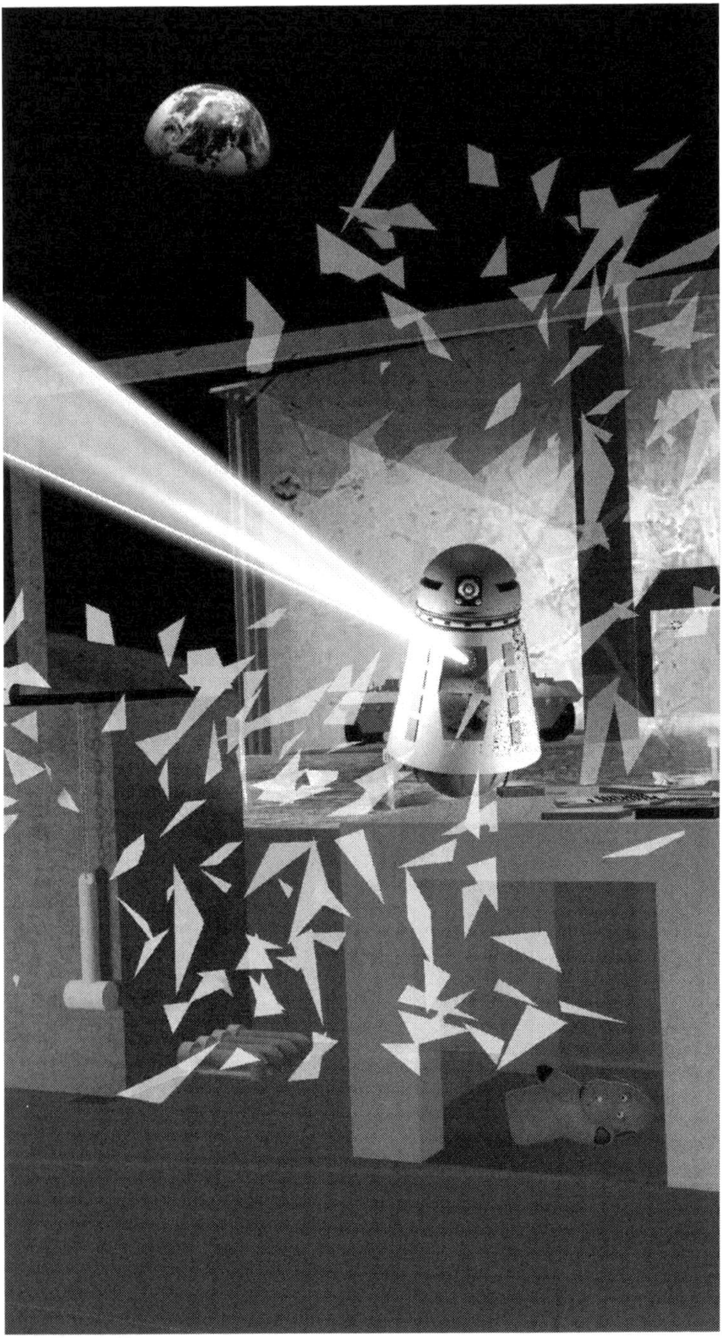

109

You hurriedly open the Orange Airlock door, and as you step into the chamber the entire Moonbase is rocked by a massive, soundless explosion. You regain your footing and slam the door shut, locking and sealing it.

The Moonbase is rocked again by a second, greater seismic blast. Daring to peer through the porthole window you're unnerved to see that the corridor outside begins to buckle and warp. In the distance, the Green Airlock flies open and a Saturmek Drone burst through at speed – as if it's running for its very life – then you watch with a mixture of horror and fascination as a large, crawling fracture in the Lunar surface swallows the Green Airlock, a portion of the corridor, the fleeing Saturmek an' all!

You've triggered a Moonquake!

Now turn to **145**.

110

Could this be a sink hole? An impact crater? An ancient magma vent? You side step to a nearby work light and flick the chunky on-switch. A football stadium-strength spotlight suddenly floods the inner shaft and you see that it's lined with perfectly smooth and symmetrical tiles. Massive metal rungs are set into the wall, like those of a colossal ladder, and they run down the depth of the shaft and into the impenetrable darkness far, far below.

As you take in the unearthly sight, it suddenly reminds you of something very work-a-day and mundane you see on a regular basis in the streets back home; and there's usually a red-and-white striped tent nearby.

"It's a manhole!" you exclaim. "It's just a perishin' great manhole made by giants!"

Looking aloft to the crane and the elevator cage that's suspended from it, it becomes evident that the crew of Moonbase Shackleton have been venturing down the shaft to the Moon's interior. It was down there that they discovered ancient, alien artefacts and secrets, and hoped to uncover much more. The elevator cage is currently level with the lip of the hole, no more than thirty feet from where you stand, awaiting the Moonbase crew to embark and descend into the depths.

"Perhaps the means of defeating the Saturmeks lies down there," you opine to yourself. "Down there, hidden in the dark, unknown depths..."

Your train of thought is rudely interrupted as an urgent message in a compelling shade of bold, red text flashes before your eyes:

ALERT: IN-SUIT AIR SUPPLY CURRENTLY AT 3%.

REPLENISHMENT ESSENTIAL IN: 0.05 HOURS.

"Wha...?! That's only about three minutes!"

You keep your breathing shallow and steady as you hurriedly turn your back on the mysterious ancient alien manhole, and the untold wonders it might contain. You must get back to the Airlock or die of suffocation!

Now turn to **134.**

111

You again glance about the chamber ever aware that time is not on your side.

If you haven't already, you might choose to take a look at – or perhaps revisit – the clear acrylic cabinet filled with spacesuits. If you want to do this, turn to **115**.

Or you might want to examine that bulky-looking Grey Airlock Door at the East end of the chamber. If this is your choice, turn to **120**.

112

The screen displays new instructions:

```
Sterilisation Protocol Alpha One needs
authorisation from one or both members of
Moonbase Shackleton's Command Team.

If both Command Team members submit their
Authorisation Code, the countdown to
detonation can be user-defined for a period
not exceeding 240 minutes.

If only one Command Team member is available
to submit their Authorisation Code, the system
must assume worse-case scenario and will
detonate immediately after arming.

Press Y to Continue. Press N to Abort.
```

Will you press the 'Y' key to continue? If so, turn to **159**.

If you've had second thoughts you can choose to press the 'N' key by turning to **105**.

113

Within Sir Clive Browne's spacious and ostentatiously decorated office, you stand on the carpet before his imposing desk flanked by Professor Wylie and Sergeant Cox. You can't help but to feel that this is like one of those prisoner-and-escort situations you see in Alcatraz movies; and you're the wayward inmate up before the Governor, about to have the kind of dressing-down that usually ends up with a spell in solitary.

After the customary minute of intimidating silence, while Sir Clive shuffles documents and signs on dotted lines as if his current task is a much more important business than you, he looks up from his paperwork.

"Thank you, Sergeant," he says brusquely. "You may leave us now."

Sergeant Cox gives a curt nod, turns on the spot and promptly exits, the heavy oak door closing behind him with a decisive thud.

"Vyvian, are you staying?" asks Sir Clive, his tone is more genial as he addresses his Departmental Head.

"I think I should on this occasion, Sir Clive," replies Professor Wylie. "Hills has been working directly under me for some time and I feel obliged."

"Very well," replies Browne as he rises from his desk and circles slowly round, hands clasping his lapels in exactly the same manner as your Form Tutor did when seriously miffed at poor mock exam results. His paces lead him to the centre of the room some few feet behind you, and you begin to turn your head to face him.

"Eyes front, Hills," whispers Professor Wylie.

Without hesitation you snap your head back to face the wall behind Sir Clive's desk, and are relieved to realise that despite her current outwardly frosty demeanour, the Professor is still in your corner.

"Professor Wylie has briefed me on the events of this morning," announces Sir Clive. "And also of your reported conduct... er... a hundred years from now. I don't think I need go into too much detail at the moment, but suffice to say that, from what has reached my ears, you displayed cowardice in the face of the enemy. What have you to say to that?"

The comment hits you hard and you feel your gut knot. Cowardice?! That's one heck of a harsh condemnation! You've never considered yourself to be lacking in courage.

Well, Hilary, what do you have to say to that? Sir Clive has given you an opportunity to explain your actions – or lack of them! – so what do you think it's best to reply with?

Will you respond;

"Sir, with respect, I'm only a civilian civil servant attached to the military. I'm a scientist, not a soldier. And I ended up on the Moonbase, in the future, entirely by accident and unprepared. I thought it was vital that I get back here alive and report my findings." If this is your choice of words, turn to **150**.

Or you might prefer to say;

"Sir Clive, I can only apologise for my inability to follow through on this occasion. I feel that my conduct was out of character, and I imagine this was a result of time-travel which, as it turns out, is disorientating and overwhelms the senses." If this is your considered reply, turn to **079**.

114

The moments pass, and all you can do is be still and think about cool, wet grass beneath your feet. Then a series of whirs and clicks echo around the inside of your helmet.

CHAMBER RECOMPRESSION COMPLETED. NORMAL EARTH ATMOSPHERE ACHIEVED. YOU MAY NOW DISROBE.

You rip the helmet off, casting it aside, and grab the locking wheel of the Red Airlock. A few determined spins see the door swing open and you're through. Taking only a moment to ensure the door closes behind you, you're off at speed.

Now turn to **199**.

115

Neatly hung in what looks like a transparent wardrobe are eight spacesuits, all of which are in pristine condition; free of dust and grime, they've evidently been thoroughly cleaned.

You open the cabinet and examine one of the suits, it's made of a tough, heavy-duty fabric the likes of which you've not seen before. This is evidently the industrial-strength outer-space work-wear worn by the Moonbase Team when they're outside doing their archaeology thing. The suits are of differing fits and sizes, tailor-made for each crew member, the names of who are displayed on their chest-patches:

King, Rex. (Cdr), Lawson, Claire. (Lt), Taylor, Symes., Atasiei, Minodora., Petkovic, Franz., Amphlett, Jon., Murrenmaw, Morgana., Ricketts, Tim. (Med).

You indulge yourself with a fleeting moment of sombre introspection as you learn the names of the people who lived... died... here.

The spacesuits look very cumbersome. It's highly unlikely that anybody wearing one would be able to out run or outmanoeuvre a Saturmek!

Do you feel you need one? Should you put one on?

If you want to get decked-out in a full spacesuit, then turn to **148**.

If you think this is unnecessarily risky, what with the Saturmeks an' everything, and would rather stay agile and mobile, then turn to **029**.

116

You find walking in one-sixth Earth gravity, in a *proper* pressurised spacesuit, isn't as easy as Fairfax and Cardew made it look on telly.* And they didn't have the advantage of 21st Century technology, you note, hearing the clicking and whirring of little servomotors within your garment which seem to compensate for every potential misstep and clumsy lurch you almost make.

"Walking in these clunky boots isn't helping," you mutter to yourself. "More of a plimsoll person, me."

Now turn to **107**.

---

* This, of course, refers to Flight Lieutenant Deirdre Fairfax and Wing Commander Percival Cardew, the first people to walk on the Moon, 3rd June 1969. See the Acknowledgement section at the rear of this book for more information.

117

You bound, as best you can, across the Lunar surface, eyes darting left and right as you consider your options.

Do you head over to the garage for a closer look at the vehicles? If so, turn to **107**.

Or do you take a short skip and a hop to investigate the nearby Hut? To do this, turn to **140**.

118

Moments later you are back where you first arrived on Moonbase Shackleton; the large Orange Airlock Door. With circumspect, you follow the simple three-step door-opening guide as before.

The door swings outward, driven by entirely silent motors, and you step hastily into the small chamber.

The Airlock door seals itself behind you, and you dare a quick glance through the porthole to ensure you weren't spotted or followed. Reassuringly, no Saturmeks are to be seen or heard in the vicinity. You know that they're doing their business mostly at the North end of Shackleton and discovery is the least of your worries.

"Hurry, Professor," you mutter as you turn your back on the door and crouch out of sight. "You've got about three minutes!"

Now turn to **170**.

119

Exiting the Truck and Container Garage, and now facing West, you see that just a short walk directly ahead of you is the caravan-sized kiosk.

But if you were to turn on your heel and head East for about 100 yards you could investigate the large crane structure and the circle of lights. From this vantage point you can see that suspended from the crane on a thick cable is what looks like an elevator cage. It's also now apparent that the lights run around the circumference of a very large hole in the Moon's surface over which the cabin hangs. This is clearly the main area of excavation.

Will you nip across to the kiosk-like shed? If so, turn to **140.**

Or will you bounce and hop a hundred yards over the Lunar surface to investigate the crane, elevator cage and hole? To do this, turn to **129.**

120

You approach the grey, windowless, sturdy-looking door; a massive, circular bulkhead portal of perhaps eight feet diameter. The orange beacon set into the wall above it looks like the type of flashing light you'd expect to see on a breakdown recover truck... only it's not flashing, or even lit for that matter.

"Distractions! Concentrate, Hills!" You mutter.

The door has massive hinges on the left, a chunky locking mechanism on the right, and in the middle of the door is a screen the size of a paperback book with a small keypad beneath it. You can see the screen is switched on because it's illuminated dark blue and has a single line of white writing which reads ENTER LOGIN, followed by a blinking underline.

Above the screen is an A4 sheet of paper, laminated and held in place by strips of adhesive tape, which contains a significant amount of typeset writing.

The lack of window makes it impossible for you to determine whether this really is an Airlock which leads to the outside, or an internal bulkhead door leading to another section of the Moonbase.

There are Saturmeks at large, and you could be discovered at any moment, so do you really have the time to read the wordy A4 poster? If you think you do, then turn to **158.**

If you would prefer to forge ahead, and not risk wasting time, you can try entering a LOGIN. To do this, turn to **094.**

121

The low gravity means climbing is surprisingly easy, and you make short work of clambering up the forty-odd feet of cable to scramble onto the gargantuan chair's armrest.

Now, standing on the ten-feet wide platform, which seems to be cast from the same smooth, concrete-like material as the floor, you can appreciate the simple design of the control pad over which the pilot's enormous withered hand is eternally poised. There's a joystick, rather like the ones on arcade video game machines, but it's the size of a tree-trunk, there are a few other paving slab-sized buttons, and located centrally is a circular silver plate with a square hole in it, which looks to you uncannily like where you'd stick an ignition key. You're not even going try to understand exactly how the Moon was once flown by poor ol' Ramesses here, but it's enough to confirm – as far as you can – that he did the job sat in this chair.

And if the Saturmeks intend to start the long-dormant engines of this huge ship and crash it into Earth, they'll need to do it from this control panel.

You decide that blowing up the chair is your best chance at scuppering their diabolical plot!

Now turn to **165.**

122

Perhaps, if you were somehow able to climb up to the giant's armrest, where you can see there's a big lever, and presumably other control knobs and switches, you might be able to...

Your desperate and impractical ruminations are suddenly interrupted by a now annoyingly familiar burst of text appearing before your eyes.

Turn to **104**.

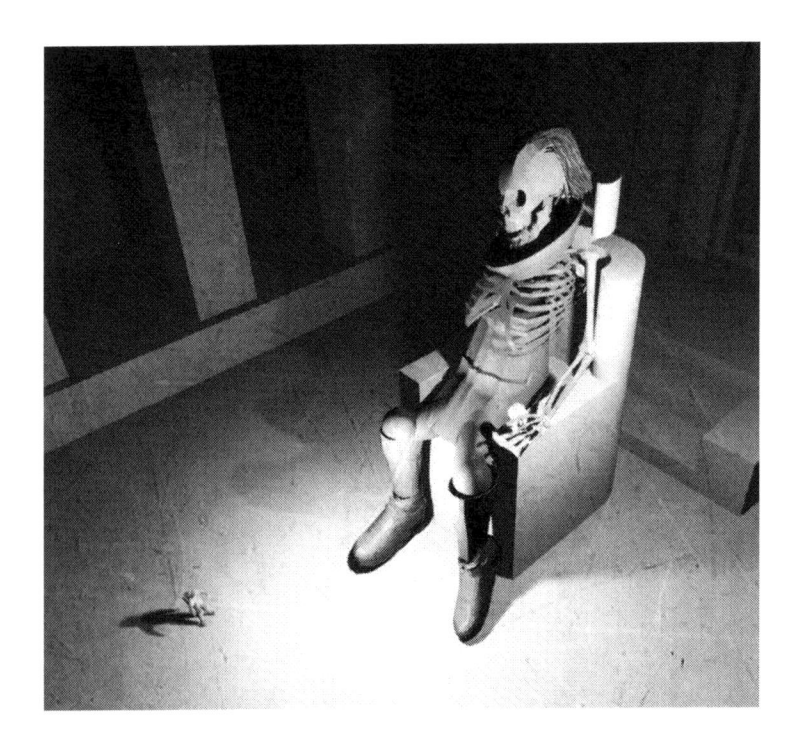

123

Stood at the Land Rover-sized left, booted and dusty foot of the dead pilot, you slowly turn a full circle looking for any and all signs of Moonbase Shackleton technology that the crew might have brought down. You see the bank of generators, the cables that lead to-and-from them, and the numerous strategically-positioned floodlights that they power... but nothing else.

There's no sign of a chunky space-age computer with a big red button labelled *Self Destruct*. You'd expected to see a Sterilisation Protocol Alpha One console installed down here, to stop an emergent threat at the source, so to speak.

You let out a huff of dismay, and turn your eyes upwards towards the face of the dead alien colossus, noting with gallows humour that his gawping expression – blank eyes, mouth opened slightly, head tilted to one side – pretty much matches how you feel at the moment.

"It's fortunate that you had the presence of mind to park your big, round spaceship in orbit as you sat there dying," you voice aloud to the ancient corpse, a habit of yours to dispel anxiety, "rather than smash into Mother Earth. Were you friends to the people of Earth? Did you flood your ship with radiation to kill a lethal virus? Were you protecting us as you died at the controls? Hey, hang on, you died at the..."

Your voice trails off as a brilliant idea occurs to you.

Now turn to **103**.

124

From your hiding place, you can see a workstation up against the North wall. This workstation is essentially a wide, narrow desk of a height that suggests it's designed to be stood at, rather than occupied by someone seated. You see four keyboards on the desk, each positioned in front of a monitor screen. In the subdued light of the Operations Centre, the displays on the screens are easy to discern. You also note that the desk is cluttered with various items.

Among the sundry bric-a-brac that appears to have been unceremoniously dumped on the desk are a number of compact, hand-held gadgets that resemble the Sinclair Scientific Calculator you use at SItU, but you imagine these are far more technically advanced than your model. There are also a few slightly larger, flatter devices which look to be all-screen and no buttons. Near the edge of the desk, you spy a forlorn-looking plush toy, which you recognise as *Sweep* from *The Sooty Show,* and you guess the cuddly toy was the lucky mascot of a crewmember. You assume the Saturmeks gathered these various items whilst rummaging through the crew's personal property and, having found nothing of use, have contemptuously discarded them.

The monitor on the left shows what you think must be a live camera feed. The image is a little snowy with static, but appears to be of a large room viewed from a high angle. In the middle of the room, slumped in a chair which resembles a throne, is a mummified corpse.

The monitor immediately next to it displays a screen of text which reads: *There were giants in the earth in those days; - Genesis 6:4.* Below the paragraph, in smaller text, someone has made a few footnotes. The comments are too small to read clearly, but you discern the words *Nephilim*, and *still present* in bold text.

The third monitor shows a portrait photo of an attractive woman, probably in her mid-thirties, with a practical, short haircut and mischievous smile. Alongside the picture is message, a communication from this woman to her superior, which reads:

```
Rex, can you look into something for me? Just
come off night-shift, saw a craft fly over.
Looked to be landing near crater. Couldn't ID.
Probably a wayward supply drone. If you need
me, wake me.
```

The last monitor shows a photo of a ruggedly good-looking man, in his early fifties, with greying hair swept back from his temples, and a jawline of salt-and-pepper stubble. Onscreen text states that this is Rexford Donald King, Moonbase Commander, and is followed by a list of personal information. The Saturmeks have accessed the databanks to ensure all the crew are accounted for.

Now turn to **172**.

125

Should you climb into the elevator cage and take a ride down into the depths of this Ancient Alien Well? If you choose to do so, turn to **168**.

Or do you think you might be going off half-cocked, and perhaps a more thorough investigation of what's up here could prove more useful? In this is the case, turn to **117**.

126

You have no desire to hang around, and so run, stumble and bounce across the Lunar surface towards the Grey Airlock, all the time hearing your spacesuit's internal servomotors fighting vigorously to keep you upright.

A breathless and muscle-aching minute later, you stumble through the Grey windowless Airlock Door and back into the Decompression Chamber. Your eyes dart about the Airlock doorframe hoping to see a lever or switch marked *Close Door with This*, then you spot a green illuminated button set into the chunky locking mechanism on the right, and so punch it. The orange beacon begins to flash as the Airlock door gracefully, but slowly, swings closed.

The video screen on the now-secured door lights up...

CHAMBER RECOMPRESSION INITIATED. RECOMPRESSING... 60.

The on-screen digit promptly changes to 59, then 58, 57, as it counts down the one-minute-long recompression procedure.

Hastily you cross the chamber to the Red Airlock on the West side, keen to return to the relative safety of the Orange Airlock. You try to spin the locking wheel, but it seems to be jammed! Removing this restrictive suit might help, you think, so you grasp the helmet and attempt to take it off, but the darn thing won't budge!

HELMET REMOVAL PROHIBITED UNTIL EARTH-NORMAL ATMOSPHERE DETECTED, explains the suit with helpful in-visor text.

"Bugger it," you gasp. "That explains why I can't open the airlock either. But I'm running out of time!"

Now turn to **114**.

127

A video monitor and keyboard hydraulically rise up from within the cabinet. The screen flickers into life, displaying lime green text on a black background which, for the sake of absolute clarity, you read aloud to yourself:

"Sterilisation Protocol Alpha One is an absolute last resort solution. It must only be initiated in the event of an insurmountable threat to Earth security.

When initiated, the protocol will begin a user-defined or predefined countdown to detonate a four-part fusion-boosted fission device situated in key areas about Moonbase Shackleton and environs.

On detonation, the Moonbase and a surrounding area of one-quarter mile will be atomised, leaving only a sterile environment.

Do you wish to continue? Y/N."

Will you press the 'Y' key to continue? If so, turn to **154**.

But if you're had second thoughts, and this all sounds too drastic and final, then you can choose to press the 'N' key by turning to **149**.

128

You first impressions are of a pounding headache, a rhythmic pressure on your chest, and the strange taste and aroma of rubber. You open your eyes and find yourself staring at the wide, vaulted ceiling of the Decompression Chamber. You're flat on your back, you can't move your head, and you can't sit up.

"The prisoner has revived," states a dreadful electronic voice. "You may desist in the chest compressions."

You swivel your eyes and bring a Green Saturmek Drone into focus as it disconnects its suction-cup appendage from your breast bone and retracts the utility arm back into its trunk. You realise the Drone is accompanied by a Blue cohort, which has its own rubbery suction-cup attachment secured over your nose and mouth; its using it to feed you air like an oxygen mask!

You raise a hand and try to feebly knock the plunger attachment away.

"You no longer require assistance breathing?" the Blue-domed Saturmek Scientist asks.

"Nmmmph!" You reply, shaking your head the slight amount that the firm grasp of the plunger will allow.

The Scientist complies, retracting its telescopic limb, freeing you from its rubbery grip.

"You will stand," barks the Drone.

With considerable aches, pains and cramps, you manage to comply, then you realise that you've been stripped of your spacesuit, and your top is torn open.

"You... gave me... CPR?!"

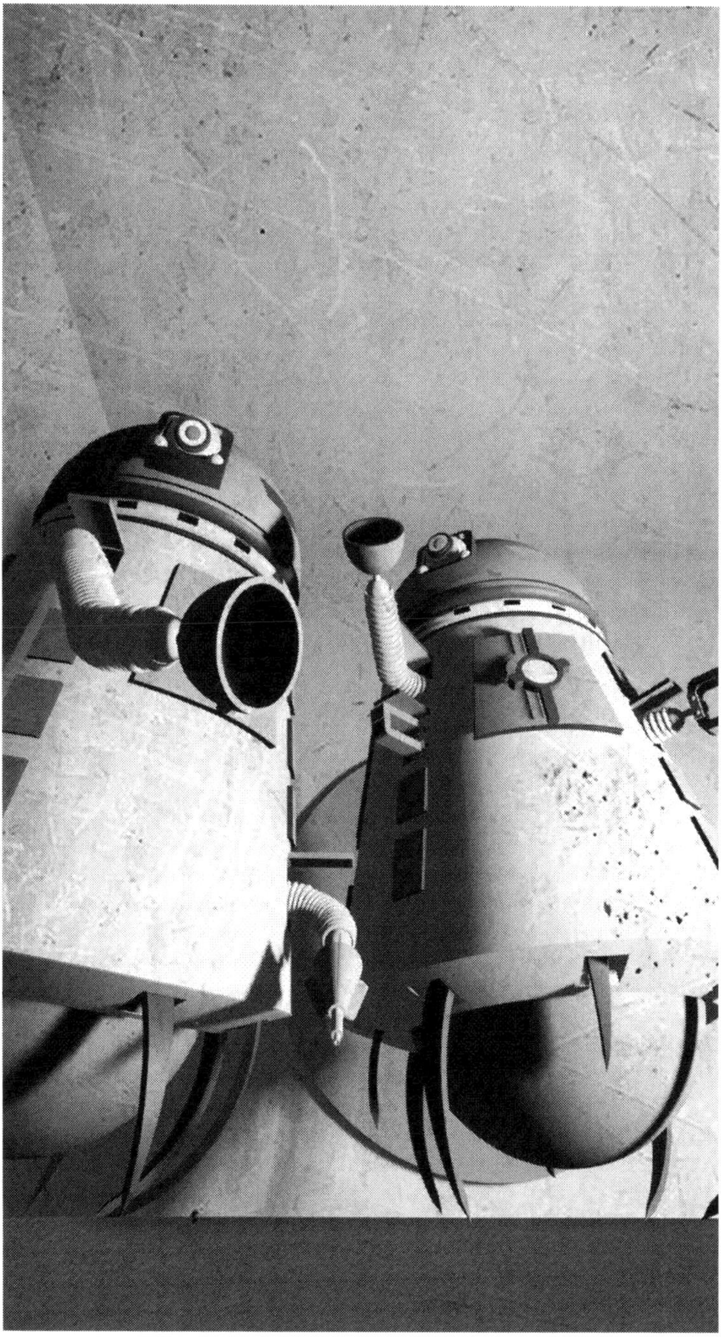

"You were dying," replies the Drone factually. "We saved you."

You can barely believe what you're hearing; Saturmeks are not generally known for their paramedic skills.

"I have a comprehensive knowledge of human biology," adds the Scientist. "Having dissected many of your kind."

Now turn to **003**.

129

Slowly, but with increasing steadiness and confidence, you half-walk and half-bunny hop along the light-pole lined pathway to the main excavation area. As you near the illuminated chasm in the ground you begin to appreciate the scale and significance of it; a geometrically perfect circular hole, probably no less than forty feet in diameter, bored straight into the Moon's bedrock. A number of tripod-mounted work lights are placed thither-and-yon, a few are switched on. You approach with caution until you're just a few short steps from the edge of this gaping maw.

Now turn to **110**.

130

Keeping low, you creep from behind the bank of computer terminals and skulk across to the Stone Needle Artefact in the middle of the room, keeping an eye on the Saturmeks at all times.

Recalling the Operational Directions you browsed earlier, you decide to use the analogue timers to set the mines to detonate, hoping that the clockwork tick of the countdown is discreet enough not to be heard by the assembled, and currently oblivious, Saturmeks.

Using the self-adhesive strips, you attached both mines to the side of the Artefact facing away from the preoccupied fiends and then prime each mine by twisting the timer dial to its half of its fullest extent; 300. You reckon the measurement must be in seconds, so it should be just five minutes until... *boom!*

You really have no clue how powerful these explosives are, but assume they were used by the Moonbase Shackleton Archaeologists for blasting Lunar rock during their excavations, so you guess they must be pretty potent. The blast will certainly destroy the Lunar Artefact, hopefully destroy the Saturmeks, and probably demolish some of the infrastructure of the base. Let's face it; you've just set the countdown to something that's very likely to cause a great deal of carnage, catastrophic decompression, and probably the total destruction of this segment of the Moonbase!

Again crawling on your hands and knees, you scurry the short distance back to the double doors and slip deftly through, unnoticed by the busy Saturmeks.

Add 25 points to your Savvy Score and turn to **171**.

131

You study the alpha-numerical keypad; letters A to Z, numbers 0 to 9, and numerous symbols. With a huff of contempt, you resign yourself to the fact that, although Professor Wylie could probably crack the code in a few minutes, you could be stabbing at the keypad for months and still get no closer to opening the door. You resist the urge to enter a random number to see what happens, suspecting that invalid codes might cause an alarm to sound.

Turning your back on the resolutely locked door you give the chamber one last quick look-over before deciding there is little of use to you here.

If you're decked-out in a spacesuit, then you feel it's far too cumbersome to continue wearing and would much rather continue to sneak about the Moonbase in your *civvies*. Thankfully, removing it proves to be just as quick and easy as putting it on.

You then stride with renewed determination across the chamber and to the exit.

Now turn to **177**.

132

The descending cage decelerates notably. You look down through the lattice-work floor again and see a myriad of lights flicker into life a few hundred feet below you... and closing. Then, quite abruptly, the seemingly endless vertical blur of tiles ends and the cage descends into a flood-lit chamber containing such sights as to take your breath away.

The elevator slows to a halt a few inches above a perfectly flat, smooth floor which might be concrete or something similar, but is definitely manufactured. Stepping out of the cage, you plant your booted foot firmly onto ancient alien territory, and look about in awe.

"Just one small step for Hilary Hills..."

The scale of this chamber is almost too much to fathom; the floor stretches out before you like an airport runway, the walls flank you like towering sky-scrapers, but you manage to gain a sense of perspective when you imagine yourself as a mouse sneaking from out of the hole in the skirting and into the manor house kitchen.

Looking directly ahead, it becomes immediately obvious from what you now see that this vast chamber must be the Pilot's Cockpit of Spaceship Moon.

Now turn to **142.**

133

You prime each mine, twisting the timer dial to its fullest extent; 600. You gather that the measurement is time in seconds, so it's just ten minutes until... *boom!*

You do some rough-and-ready mental arithmetic; the elevator ride down took about five minutes, give-or-take, and it'll probably take another three minutes of Moon-walking between the Well Head and the Airlock.

"The clock is ticking, it's high time I got out of here," you voice to yourself.

You turn your back on the mysterious and ancient alien giant, take a deep breath and step off the edge of the structure. You don't want to hang around, clambering down the cable would take too long, and a fifty-foot drop in one-sixth Earth gravity seems like a viable option when every second counts.

Now add 27 points to your Savvy Score and turn to **144.**

134

Stumbling and bouncing across the Lunar surface, taking a breath only when absolutely necessary, you fight nausea and giddiness while your suit's internal servomotors fight with equal vigour to keep you upright.

Two breathless, muscle-aching, lung-screaming, head-rushing minutes later, you stumble through the Airlock and back into the decompression chamber.

The alarming red text flickers within your visor:

MAXIMUM ALERT: IN-SUIT AIR SUPPLY EXHAUSTED.

REPLENISHMENT ESSENTIAL IMMEDIATELY.

It's probably pure adrenaline keeping you from blacking out now, as your eyes frantically dance about the Airlock doorframe hoping to see a lever or switch marked *Close Door*. You spot a green button set into the chunky locking mechanism on the right and, in desperation, punch it.

The orange beacon begins to flash as the Airlock door swings gracefully, but oh-so slowly, closed. The video screen on the now-secured door lights up:

CHAMBER RECOMPRESSION INITIATED. RECOMPRESSING... 60.

The on-screen digit changes to 59, then 58, 57, as it counts down the minute-long recompression procedure. You struggle to remove your helmet, but it remains firmly locked to the suit and won't budge!

HELMET REMOVAL PROHIBITED UNTIL EARTH-NORMAL ATMOSPHERE DETECTED, explains the suit, with helpful in-visor text.

"Bugger," you gasp with your last breath, and then black out.

Now turn to **128.**

135

Will you now walk ahead, towards the ring of light-poles and crane structure? If so, turn to **194**.

Or will you head over to the garage for a closer look at the vehicles? If this is your choice, then turn to **116**.

Or perhaps you want to take the short walk to investigate the hut on your left? To do this, turn to **151**.

136

Then you see it; a free-standing console in the corner. This inconspicuous, waist-high, flat-topped rectangle has four cables, as thick as fire-hoses, running from out the bottom of its base and snaking away through various holes in the walls. Hanging from a chain bolted to the side of the cabinet is one of those *in-case-of-fire-break-glass* type mallets, and as you approach the console you see the flat top is smoked semi-opaque Perspex with criss-cross grooves etched deep into its surface. A large red sticker dead centre of the translucent plastic top explains, as you half-expected, everything you need to know in bold white lettering:

Sterilisation Protocol Alpha One: Command Interface Access.

Strike here to break glass.

Without hesitation you reach down and grasp the rubber-coated mallet. With one sharp and well-aimed whack you strike the sticker, and the acrylic cover shatters neatly into tiny squares.

Now turn to **127**.

137

You dare to look down, floodlights fitted to the bottom of the cage light the way, but there's no sign of the shaft's bottom yet.

PLEASE BE AWARE: IN-SUIT AIR SUPPLY CURRENTLY AT 16%.

ESTIMATED TIME UNTIL REPLENISHMENT NECESSARY: 0.51 HOURS.

The sudden flash of projected text before your eyes startles you and, once read, alarms you further.

"Only half an hour left now?!" You blurt in reply. "But I've only been out here a few minutes!"

You realise that these spacesuits are supposed to be worn by trained professionals, y'know, types who don't nearly freak-out when they find themselves in outer-space situations! You have to accept that your initial panicky gasping and frog-breathing used up a lot of your air reserve. Better keep a level head from now-on, and fixate on that cool, wet grass! Air, like time it seems, is in sort supply right now.

Now turn to **163**.

138

If you haven't already, you might consider heading over to the garage for a closer look at the vehicles. To do this, turn to **107**.

Or do you think you should head towards the ring of light-poles and crane structure to the East? If so, turn to **102**.

139

You select a locker entirely at random and, feeling for the movement of pins whilst listening intently, you begin to rotate the tumbler left and right. This is something you do with practiced ease, having mastered the art back during your schooldays; you so often forgot the combination to your own locker you'd frequently have to open it safe-cracker style.

Whirr-click... Whirr-click... Whirr-click... Whirr-clunk!

"That was a cinch," you whisper, allowing yourself a self-satisfied smile.

Now turn to **057**.

140

You approach the sturdy structure, noting the door is on the West-facing side. The door is closed, but an obvious illuminated button in the doorframe has a double-headed open-close arrow symbol on it. You thumb the button, the door promptly slides open, and once you've stepped into the caravan-sized hut it automatically closes behind you.

Looking about the small cabin it's obvious that this is the Excavation Site Manager's Office. A complicated-looking console contains countless buttons, switches and keypads, and several video screens display live feeds from the immediate area, with some being transmitted from what look to be barely-lit chambers underground. Clipboards and binders brimming with documents litter a table top, along with several hand-held computer-like thingies the purpose of which escapes you.

But you don't have time to dwell upon any of this, you're looking for something very specific, and you feel quite exposed in this flood-lit hut which is mostly all-windows!

Now turn to **136**.

141

With your back against the Red Airlock, you face East, looking out across Shackleton's Lunar archaeological excavation site. The grey terrain, powdered liberally with ashen dust of aeons, is flood-lit by several high-powered spotlights atop twenty-feet tall lampposts. Processions of shorter, dimmer lighting-poles, just twelve inches-or-so high, are laid out in a manner that indicates pathways.

One such illuminated trail leads directly ahead, stretching some one hundred and fifty yards into the distance. From your vantage point you can see this Eastwards walk terminates in a large circle of light-poles and a very tall crane-like structure.

To your right, and significantly closer than the crane, is a parking garage of rudimentary construction; an angled roof, three walls and supporting struts. Several Lunar excavating vehicles are parked there, you can see three sporty-looking two-seater space buggies, identical to the crashed vehicle you saw when you first arrived here. The other vehicles parked-up are built to far more substantial and industrial design, resembling agricultural tractors with various hydraulic attachments for heavy work, you can see a bulldozer, an arm-and-shoveler, and a driller. First impressions suggest that there's nothing of obvious interest there.

141

To your left, about forty feet from where you stand, is a hut only a little bigger than your average touring caravan. Unlike the garage, it is a sturdy-looking structure and appears to be built for permanence. Designed like a kiosk, all four walls contain large windows, giving any occupant an all-around field of view.

"That must be the Site Supervisor's Office," you muse.

Outside of the light-pole defined pathways, and dotted about the site, are exploratory trenches, cordoned off with rope barriers.

Now turn to **135.**

142

About ten years ago you went on a week-long school trip to Egypt. You spent seemingly endless days being dragged around one dusty tomb after another, by an even dustier and dour School Ma'am, and in the most uncomfortably scorching weather. It turned out that Egyptology really wasn't your thing, and the entire trip was a bust as far as you were concerned... until the last day. That was the day your class took the interminable six-hour bus ride from Luxor to Abu Simbel, but what you saw as your bus finally reached its destination blew your mind.

And now, standing here in an underground chamber on the Moon, a hundred-or-so years in the future, you can't help but to wonder if Ramesses II had somehow paid the Pilot of Spaceship Moon a visit, and immortalised what he'd seen in stone on his return to Earth. You would've once dismissed such musings as pure fancy, the result of taking Erich von Däniken a bit too seriously perhaps, but these days you're more open-minded and, of course, have read the SItU Top-Secret Files revealing that space aliens of one sort or another are visiting Earth with alarming frequency nowadays. Most are benign entities dropping in out of curiosity, or just to ask directions, and wishing to keep a very low profile. Of course, the general public know only of the Saturmeks, other extra-terrestrial encounters still being kept secret, and the Saturmeks – back in 1974, at least – are thought extinct and consigned to history.

But now, here, ahead of you, in the distance, slumped in its control chair like a long-deposed king on his throne, is seated the Moon's Pilot. Mummified by passing millennia of airless time, his dark leather skin is stretched taut over cable-like sinew and cyclopean bone, a full head of red hair, swept back from the temples, now frozen in place

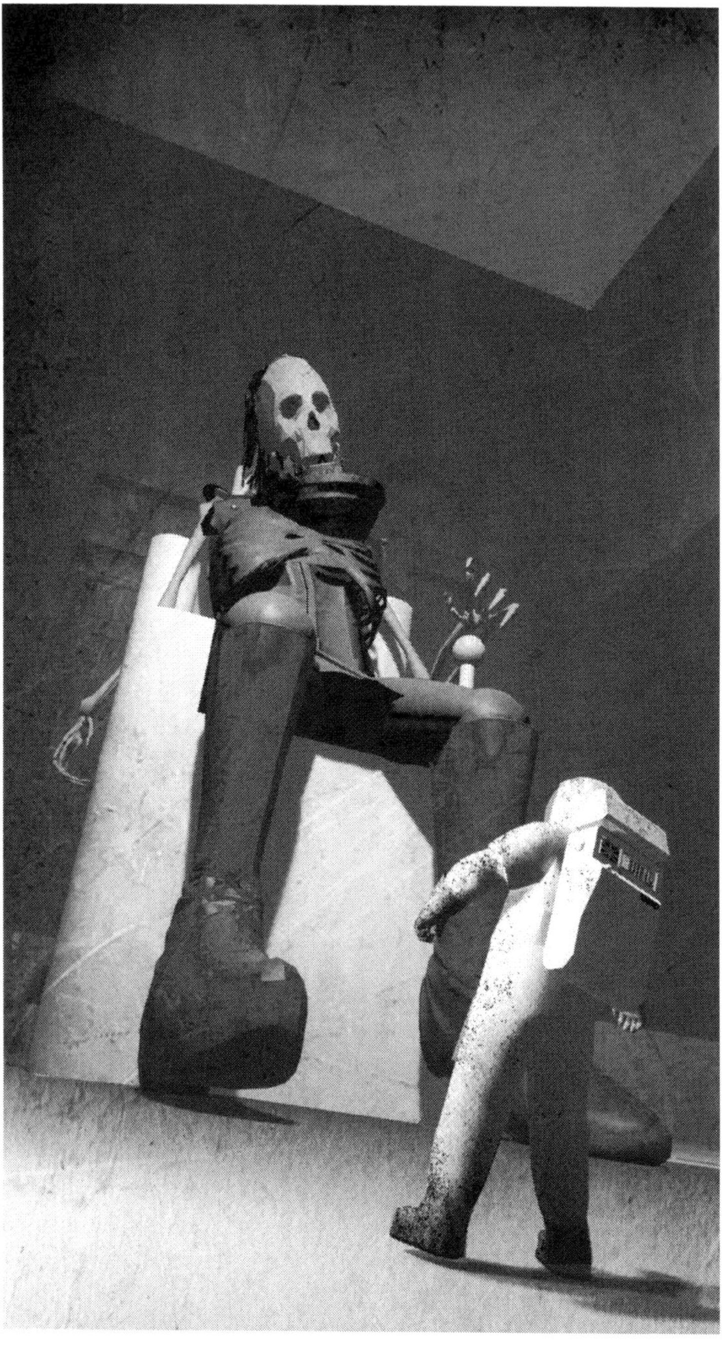

like a ginger skullcap, and a long, neatly-plaited beard lends the corpse its regal air. His tree-trunk wrists rest on the arms of his chair, his left hand still poised over a lever, frozen by death before he was able to execute some final manoeuvre.

"Blimey," you exclaim. "You're a big fella! Must be seventy feet tall."

Your suit interrupts your train of thought with a flash of information.

PLEASE BE AWARE: EXTERNAL RADIATION LEVELS HAVE INCREASED SIGNIFICANTLY.

AT CURRENT LEVELS, SUIT SHIELDING INTEGRITY AT: 100%

FOR THE NEXT: 02 HOURS

"Did a radiation leak kill you, Ramesses? I thought it was a virus?" you ask as you walk, as fast as your suit will allow, the distance of two football pitches towards the seated giant. You ignore the vast corridor that leads off to your right, you can see that it's set at an incline and presumably leads deeper into the Moon's interior, but you have no time to explore. Besides, there might be more of the dead crew down there... or worse!

Now turn to **123**.

143

A small and hither-to unnoticed panel to the right of the keyboard slides open to reveal a big, red button.

```
Priming of fusion-boosted fission devices will
commence when activation button is pressed. A
data report will be generated and transmitted
to Earth Command.

Priming Procedure and Data Transmission takes
approximately 10 seconds.

Detonation then follows immediately.

Please press the activation button now.
```

You're trembling, and it's understandable that you do, but what other choice do you have? If you don't hit that big, red button, Earth dies!

You had hoped, if only for your own satisfaction, to utter some profound last words for the ages, but nothing comes to mind so you just press the activation button.

Now turn to **160.**

144

"I can't believe I've just met the Man in the Moon," you think aloud.

The return elevator ride to the Lunar surface seems to take an eternity, but you look aloft and are relieved to see the nearing of the lights on the Moon's surface.

"That's taken up about five minutes..." you mutter.

As the crane slows the paying-in of the cable and the cage draws to a gentle halt, level with the lip of the Shackleton Well, you fix your determined gaze on the Grey Airlock Door a hundred and fifty yards across the Lunar surface.

Turn to **156**.

145

You've destroyed the Saturmeks, and Earth is safe, but you realise your heroic act has potentially come at such a cost to yourself!

Trembling, you turn your back on the fearsome sight of the encroaching chasm, and crouch into a foetal position.

"Vyvian!" You cry out. "Where are you?!"

Then you add quietly, "I'm not ready to die!"

Now turn to **155**.

146

During your brief exploration of the Moonbase so far, you discovered two explosive mining charges, which you feel you should now put to good use. Each mine, you noted at the time, had a serial number stamped onto it.

Please now add the last two digits of the first mine and the first two digits of the second mine together to result in a single figure. *

The number your arithmetic results in is the reference number you should **now turn to.**

If you are unable to do this because, through stress and fear, you mistakenly believed you possessed explosives but actually don't, then please try to clear your thoughts, go back to **050** and reconsider your situation.

For example, if you know that first mine's serial is 1234, and the second mine's serial is 5678, then you should do the following simple calculation: 34+56 which results in 100. So, in this example, you'd now turn to 100.

147

The moments pass, and all you can do is remain still and think about that cool, wet grass beneath your feet. Then a series of whirs and clicks echo around the inside of your helmet.

CHAMBER RECOMPRESSION COMPLETED. NORMAL EARTH ATMOSPHERE ACHIEVED. YOU MAY NOW DISROBE.

You rip the helmet off, casting it aside, and grab the locking wheel of the Red Airlock. A few determined spins see the door swing open and you're through, taking only a moment to ensure the door has closed behind you, you're off at speed.

Turn to **152**.

148

Atasiei's spacesuit looks to be the best fit for you. Her Crew Registration Number, which is listed under her name on the breast badge, is 1391415101. Be sure to *make a careful note of* this Crew Registration Number, just in case it's needed later.

You take it from the cabinet, pleased to see that the outer-space work-wear of the future is designed to be as easy to put on as a pair of dungarees; the boots, gauntlets, and the suitcase-sized life support backpack are all incorporated into the single garment. Keeping your own clothes on, and grateful that you pulled on your snug-fitting Chinos in preference to bell-bottoms this morning, you step into the one-piece and zip it up from crotch-to-neck. You then take the appropriate helmet, the one with the name of Mino Atasiei in bold black text above the visor, from the floor of the cabinet and place it over your head. The lipped base of the helmet meets with the wide, ribbed neck of the suit and in doing so seems to complete a circuit which seals the suit with a gentle pneumatic hiss. A short series of whirs and clicks issue from the suit as life support, temperature regulation and internal pressure systems activate.

You are momentarily startled when writing appears in front of your eyes, but you quickly realise that it's being projected onto the inside of your visor from within the helmet.

Now turn to **090.**

149

"Detonating an Atomic Bomb?!" you exclaim. "Talk about using a sledgehammer to crack a walnut!"

You're desperate to save Earth, but this brutal method might do more harm than good in the long run! You can't help thinking that Professor Wylie would whole-heartedly disapprove of this nuclear option and you feel that there must be a smarter, neater, less horrifically violent way to foil the Saturmeks' plan.

Add 20 points to your Savvy Score and turn to **105**.

150

You hear Professor Wylie let out an almost silent sigh of dismay, but keep your eyes forward.

A few moments pass as Sir Clive considers your reply, and all you hear is the carriage clock on the desk tick away the moments to his verdict.

"Civilian, Hills?" Sir Clive spits. "Is that honestly your best excuse for sitting with your thumb up your bum and your mind in neutral whilst the enemies of Earth plot its utter destruction?"

"Oh, dear," mutters Professor Wylie, and you see in your peripheral vision that her shoulders have slumped and she's lowered her head.

"It's only a matter of a few decades ago that we went up against Hitler. Too young to remember that, aren't you, Hills? The Home Guard, ARP Wardens, the WAAF, many of the Frontline Cartographers... all civilians. Selfless and courageous civilians prepared to make, if necessary, the ultimate sacrifice for the greater good of the British people. Damn it, Hills, you must know that even the initial days of the Saturmek invasion of 1897 was largely kept in check by farmers on horseback with pitchforks! Many of them were killed, but those brave wurzels bought us vital time to rally our armed forces."

Out of the corner of your eye, you see Professor Wylie straighten up and turn her head.

"Sir Clive," she interjects. "I've worked closely with Hills for some months now, often out in the field, and have never witnessed any lack of courage or moral fortitude, not even when we were faced by that ravenous horde of cannibalistic Neanderthals in Devon."

"Hurrumph," is Sir Clive's testy and unconvinced reply.

"And it was Hills that stood in a dinghy in the middle of a choppy sea and stared down the Scarborough Kraken."

"Hmm," responds Sir Clive, a little more thoughtfully. "Chucked a grenade down its gullet didn't you, Hills?"

"Yes, Sir Clive," you answer a little sheepishly, but feel your hopes of a reprieve rise.

"Were you scared then, Hilary?" asks the Professor, gently. "Answer honestly."

"Flippin' terrified!" you reply with a nervous chuckle.

"But Hills rose to the occasion and saved the crew of that trawler, Sir Clive, despite facing something that would paralyse many people with fear."

"True," replies Browne as he returns to his desk and seats himself before you like a residing judge.

"May I speculate, Sir Clive," ventures Professor Wylie, choosing her words with care, "that Hilary Hill's conduct was out of character on this occasion. I imagine this was the result of time-travel which, I expect, is extremely disorientating and overwhelming to the senses. I suspect that Hills arrived at Moonbase Shackleton in a shocked frame of mind; disassociated, and probably in a fugue state."

"I'm prepared to take what you say into account, Vyvian," replies Sir Clive. "Thank you. You may leave us now."

Professor Wylie gives you a sideways glance and offers you a sympathetic smile as she turns to leave the room. Moments later, it's just you, Sir Clive Browne, and the interminable ticking of the carriage clock.

"So, Hills," begins Browne as he arches his back and squares his shoulders. "To your credit we now know that the Saturmeks are still at large out there in space. We had hoped the germ bombs devised back in '97 had finished them off for good, but always suspected that there might be a few survivors that escaped. It's a pity that current rocket technology doesn't allow us to take the fight to them, but at least it seems we have decades to prepare."

Sir Clive pauses and takes his time to look you up and down, as if even now he's considering his verdict. Cowardice, he had said, and you wonder if he still holds that opinion of you.

"To your detriment, however, you failed to undertake any meaningful action against a present and obvious enemy when the opportunity presented itself. This dereliction of duty was, I believe, very much out of keeping with your usual character, and was the result of... well, I suppose from Vyvian's observations, we could call it shell-shock."

Sir Clive reaches for the telephone, his finger dials a simple two-digit number as he presses the receiver to his ear. The discreet, almost murmured conversation he has is brief; you only catch the name Doctor Gardner, the word *evaluation* and the phrase *yes, right now, Peter*. Browne replaces the receiver and rises to his feet again.

"Did you catch any of that, Hills?" he asks.

"Not a word, Sir," you half-truth.

"I'm not going to hold you responsible for your inaction against enemy forces. Professor Wylie thinks that the balance of your mind was disturbed, and I trust her counsel."

"Thank you, Sir Clive," you gasp with relief.

"However," Browne is quick to reply, an index finger raised for emphasis. "I am discharging you of all your duties for the foreseeable future. Doctor Gardner will be here imminently to take charge of you, and whilst in his care you will undergo a thorough psychiatric assessment and receive all appropriate treatment."

A stocky, grey-haired, grey-bearded, lab-coated man enters the office without bothering to knock.

"Good morning, Peter," greets Sir Clive. "This is Hilary Hills, whom I'm placing into your care. Please liaise with Professor Wylie before lunch, she can fill you in on all the details."

Sir Clive saves his last words on the subject for you, folding his arms and leaning back in his chair, he looks pointedly into your eyes.

"Only when – and *if* – Doctor Gardner deems you fit to resume your duties will you return to the workplace."

You have no choice but to comply with Sir Clive's edict, but this feels like such an ignominious fate, and you know that if you could live this morning all over again, you'd definitely do things differently.

The End.

151

You find walking in one-sixth Earth gravity, in a *proper* pressurised spacesuit, isn't as easy as Fairfax and Cardew made it look on telly.* And they didn't have the advantage of 21st Century technology, you note, hearing the whirr of little servomotors within your garment which seem to compensate for every misstep and clumsy lurch you take.

"Walking in these clunky boots isn't helping," you mutter to yourself. "More of a moccasins person, me."

Now turn **140**.

* This, of course, refers to Flight Lieutenant Deirdre Fairfax and Wing Commander Percival Cardew, the first people to walk on the Moon, 3rd June 1969. See the Acknowledgement section at the rear of this book for more information.

152

Although you fear the Saturmeks, you fear being blown to pieces or sucked out into space more, and so sprint up the East Corridor with reckless abandon. Although your spacesuit now hangs baggily about your frame, it doesn't impede your frantic gait as you take a sharp left at the junction and barrel down the Central Corridor towards the Green Airlock.

Knowing that it can now be only a matter of mere minutes before the excavation site explodes, you're through the Green Airlock in moments and darting towards the Orange Airlock where you originally fell arse-backwards into this nightmare.

Turn to **109**.

153

During your brief exploration of the Moonbase so far, you discovered two explosive mining charges, which you stuffed in a satchel and have carried with you, slung over your shoulder, ever since. Even when you clambered into this spacesuit, you had the presence of mind not to leave your precious *bag full o' bombs* behind! You feel it's now time to put this lethal ordinance to good use. Each mine, you noted at the time, had a serial number stamped onto it.

Please now add the middle two digits of the first mine and the middle two digits of the second mine together to result in a single figure. *

The number your arithmetic results in is the page you should **now turn to.**

If you are unable to do this because, through stress and fear, you mistakenly believed you possessed explosives but actually don't, then please try to clear your thoughts, go back to **103** and reconsider your situation.

---

* For example, if you know that first mine's serial is 1234, and the second mine's serial is 5678, you should do the following simple calculation: 23+67 which results in 90. So, in this example, you'd now turn to 90.

154

"Detonating an Atomic Bomb?!" you exclaim. "Talk about using a sledgehammer to crack a walnut!"

But you're desperate to protect the Earth, and this brutal measure will save billions of lives... and your very planet!

You hit the 'Y' key because, you tell yourself, sometimes the ends really do justify the means.

Now turn to **112**.

155

Suddenly, as if in response to your frantic plea, that longed-for shimmering ball light reappears in the middle of the room, accompanied by the thunderous crackle of raw, ethereal energy.

From cricket ball, through football, the light phases and pulses. Then it grows rapidly to a size that fills half the chamber as it morphs into the now-welcome sight of a horizontal tornado of swirling, spinning plasma and lightning. A familiar voice, as clear as a bell, issues from deep within the vaporous funnel...

"Hills! I can see you," says Professor Wylie, with relief evident in her voice. "Can you see me?"

You peer into the heart of the Fugacious Spatial Vortex, having to squint against the harshness of the light, and there, in a giddying and weird sort of way, you see the Professor stood in the middle of her laboratory at SItU Headquarters. She seems to be about ten feet and a million miles away from you simultaneously.

"Professor! Get me out of here!" you cry frantically.

"Run towards me, Hilary, and quickly, I can't keep it open much longer. Be sure to duck, I don't want you to arrive home without your head!"

Without any further hesitation you run towards the tunnel of blue light, ducking at the last moment.

For a few brief moments you're tumbling, weightlessly, intangibly, and seemingly downwards, through a tunnel of twisting blue-green light, and then...

...you fall into Professor Wylie's arms.

"Easy, Hills, I got you," you immediately hear her say, in her calm, reassuring tone.

For a moment you can still hear the crackle of raw, angry vortex energy, and then a loud bang as sparks and smoke fountain from out of the salvaged time-travel engine like a roman candle. You and the Professor watch together as the Fugacious Spatial Vortex flickers and fades.

Professor Wylie grabs a small fire extinguisher from her lab-bench and crosses to the crackling, flaring machinery. With just a few skillfully-directed blasts of CO_2 she brings the sparking and smouldering under control.

"Such a pity," she mutters sulkily. "Took me half-an-hour of frantic work to reassemble the Berwyn Device and get it operational. Probably beyond salvaging now."

The Professor, frowning and pouting like a petulant child, then turns her attention to you.

"You alright, Hilary?" Wylie's query is brusque.

"Yeah, I'll be okay," you reply. "Professor, I was on..."

"A Moonbase, one hundred years in the future, I gathered as much from the view the vortex gave me of the airlock, Hills," interrupts the Professor. "You know, you should never have put the battery in that Temporal Condenser Circuit you were working on. I'd just started to tweak the settings in the very heart of the Tachyon Capacitor, you see, so once you'd turned the Temporal Condenser on your fate was sealed."

You stare at the Professor, rather nonplussed by her explanation, and feeling very hurt and dismayed at her scalding. Professor Wylie sees the pain in your eyes and her expression immediately softens to one earnest concern as she slowly approaches and, with a somewhat awkward demeanour, takes your hands in hers.

"You're quite ashen and – goodness gracious! – you're trembling," she says softly.

"What d'you expect? I fell through time! To the Moon!" You try to sound angry, but with all you've been through it sounds more like a mewle of disbelief.

"Y'know... ah... actually..." stumbles Professor Wylie. "It's probably my fault you ended up there; my carelessness that caused the localised Temporal-Spatial Distortion. I'm sorry, Hills."

"Saturmeks," you reply, and are unsure what else to add until you blurt. "They're going to destroy the Earth!"

"Saturmeks? Really? Look, Hilary, I'm a bit fuzzy on physical laws of time, but I do know that what you've just witnessed, no matter how immediate and raw it seems to you, hasn't happened yet. In fact, it won't happen for a hundred years... if it happens at all."

The Professor's voice trails off with a heavy sigh. You can see by the distant look in her eyes, and the way she nervously twiddles her necklace, that the thought of the terrifying experience you've undergone has just sunk in.

"Well, the Earth of here and now is under no imminent threat, that's the main thing," finishes the Professor disjointedly as she snaps out of her reverie. "Perhaps the return of the Saturmeks in the year 2074 is historical fact... er, future historical fact... that is to say, but it hasn't happened yet, and is a merely speculative future, but perhaps it will happen, and once it has happened, it will be fixed in history... er... If you get my meaning."

You can't help but to smile at Professor Wylie's fumbling exposition, and with the lifting of your spirits you realize that you're home and safe.

"Why don't you try to explain it to me again, over a nice big mug of sweet tea in the NAAFI," you suggest warmly.

"Hm, yes," the Professor grins. "I think a cup of tea and a slice of cake would..."

Professor Wylie pauses mid-sentence whilst looking you up and down quizzically.

"Just a minute... Is that a spacesuit you're wearing, Hills?"

Now turn to the Epilogue at **200**.

156

Running, stumbling and bouncing across the Lunar surface, you fight growing feelings of fear and dread while your suit's internal servomotors fight with equal vigour to keep you upright.

A breathless and muscle-aching minute later, you stumble through the Grey Airlock Door and back into the spacious Decompression Chamber. Your eyes frantically dance about the Airlock doorframe hoping to spot a lever or switch marked *Close Door*. You see a green illuminated button set into the chunky locking mechanism on the right, and so in desperation punch it. The orange beacon begins to flash as the Airlock door gracefully, but slowly, swings closed.

The video screen on the now-secured door lights up...

CHAMBER RECOMPRESSION INITIATED. RECOMPRESSING... 60.

The on-screen digit promptly changes to 59, then 58, 57, as it counts down the one-minute-long recompression procedure.

You hastily cross the chamber to the Red Airlock on the West side, wanting to put as much distance between you and the imminent explosion as possible. You try to spin the locking wheel, but it seems to be jammed! Removing this restrictive suit might help, you think, so you grasp the helmet and attempt to remove it, but it won't budge!

HELMET REMOVAL PROHIBITED UNTIL EARTH-NORMAL ATMOSPHERE DETECTED, explains the suit with helpful in-visor text.

"Bugger it," you gasp. "That explains why I can't open the Airlock either. But I'm running out of time!"

Turn to **147**.

157

As you take the unearthly sight in, it suddenly reminds you of something very work-a-day and mundane you see on a regular basis in the streets back home; and there's usually a red-and-white striped tent nearby.

"It's a manhole!" you exclaim. "It's just a bloomin' great manhole made for giants!"

Looking aloft to the crane and the elevator cage suspended from it, it becomes evident that the crew of Moonbase Shackleton have been venturing down the shaft and into the Moon's interior. It was down there that they discovered ancient alien artefacts and secrets, and hoped to uncover so much more. The elevator cage is currently level with the lip of the hole, no more than thirty feet from where you stand, awaiting the Moonbase crew to embark and descend into the depths.

"Perhaps the means of defeating the Saturmeks lies down there," you opine to yourself. "Down there, hidden in the dark, unknown depths…"

You carefully make your way around the hole to the elevator cage. It's a very basic design, and brings to mind those used by coal miners in Wales. You see that the elevator is controlled by a couple of simple go–stop and up–down levers.

"Looks straight-forward enough," you reassure yourself. "But, oh, such a long way down!"

Now turn to **125.**

158

You scan over the text, speed-reading several preamble paragraphs of legalese waffle and rubber-stamp Health & Safety clauses. Then you come to some rather more relevant information, helpfully presented as curt bullet-points in a bold and slightly larger text.

Door leads to Lunar surface.

Spacesuits must be worn by all personnel present in chamber during ingress or egress of work party.

No solo working under any circumstances. Mandatory minimum work party of three personnel to operate on Lunar surface at any time.

Work party must consist of at least one Moonbase Senior.

Current Seniors on roster:

Commander Rexford Donald King (dayshift)

Lieutenant Claire Delune Lawson (nightshift).

Chamber will decompress in 60 seconds, and door will open, when a Moonbase Senior activates LOGIN by entering their Authorisation Code.

"Hmm. Good to know," you comment.

Add 10 points to your Savvy Score.

Will you now try entering a LOGIN? If so, turn to **094**.

Or will you take a look, perhaps a second look, at the nearby spacesuits? If so, turn to **115**.

159

The screen displays new instructions:

```
Are both members of the Moonbase Shackleton
Command Team present to submit their
Authorisation Codes?

Enter Y/N.
```

Are you in possession of both Authorisation Codes, or do you know just one?

If you know just one code then turn to **106**.

If you have both codes, turn to **166**.

160

The screen displays a final string of messages:

```
Gathering data.

Transmitting data.

Arming fusion-boosted fission devices.

Your selfless act of sacrifice ensures the
continued safety of Earth and every soul upon
her.

Godspeed.

Devices armed in 10... 09... 08...
```

"When I lay me down to die, Goin' up to the spirit in the sky..." You sing tearfully, finding some comfort in the words while waiting to be atomised.

Now turn to **108**.

161

"I thought once you'd seen one Airlock, you'd seen them all," you think aloud as you look around the brightly-lit, impressively large, vaulted chamber. Then you hastily turn and ensure the door shuts and seals behind you. Although living very much on your nerves at the moment, you feel a little safer with the huge door firmly closed as you again turn about to survey the room in detail.

You stand at the West end of a large chamber, which you estimate is about ten feet wider than the corridor from which you entered, with a substantially higher, vaulted ceiling. It's clearly fabricated from the same materials as the other areas of the Moonbase you've visited, but in comparison to the stark and functional environment of Shackleton in general, this room appears to be positively luxurious.

You can see a row of metal personal lockers, neatly-stored spacesuits, a communal shower, a large food dispenser, a comfy and generously proportioned sofa, a television set with a screen bigger than anything you thought possible, four chaises longues, and a bookcase filled with literature and what might be audio cassettes. This place looks more like an up-market rec room or, more likely, an Officers' Mess, than an Airlock!

In fact, the only reason you think this might be an Airlock is the single, windowless and formidable-looking circular Grey Door set into the wall the other end of the room. There's clearly a notice on this door, but the text is too small to read from where you're standing.

Now turn to **019.**

162

Your fingers hover over the keypad below the blue screen, as you recall the Authorisation Code you learnt earlier.

If you have acquired multiple different Authorisation Codes during your adventure, please choose just one. Any one will do; whichever immediately come to mind.

But if, through fear and anxiety, you realise to your dismay that you have since forgotten any Authorisation Codes you might have learnt earlier (or perhaps you are simply mistaken, and didn't acquire any at all) then you should now turn to **131.**

Here's how to enter your Authorisation Code as a LOGIN: Add all the individual digits of the code together to give you a total. *

The total is the reference you should **now turn to.**

---

* For example, if the code is 12345, then do the following sum: 1+2+3+4+5, which adds up to a total of 15. So, 15 would be the reference you would now turn to in this example.

163

"I am barefoot," you intone. "Standing on cool, dewy sod. In a fragrant meadow. On a balmy springtime morn."

As if in reply, your suit flickers another message onto the inside of your visor.

PLEASE BE AWARE: EXTERNAL RADIATION LEVELS INCREASING.

AT CURRENT LEVELS, SUIT SHIELDING INTEGRITY AT: 100%

FOR THE NEXT: 05 HOURS

"I must be barmy," you exclaim.

The cage continues in its speedy descent, as the precious minutes tick by.

Now turn to **132**.

164

Despite the restrictions imposed on your movement by your spacesuit, you find that swinging and launching the tripod upwards in one-sixth gravity is surprisingly easy. In fact, it overshoots the armrest by several feet, but arcs over as it descends, hits its mark and wraps repeatedly around the arm under its own momentum. You tug at the cable, and with a sense of great satisfaction you determine that it's securely lassoed to the structure. Then, without hesitation, and knowing all that's at stake, you begin to scale the cable.

"Some people call me the Space Cowboy..." you sing to bolster your courage as you climb.

Add 10 points to your Savvy Score and turn to **121**.

165

If your guess is correct, then this control panel is used to fly the Moon, so destroying it should permanently put an end to the Saturmeks' genocidal plans. You take the two hemispherical mines from your satchel and study them with grim determination. You have no desire to die, but the Saturmeks' planet-killing plan must be stopped. Here alone, you can see no other option but to risk your life to save billions.

"Sorry, Ramesses," you say, glancing up to the lifeless face some thirty-odd feet above you. "It's been nice to meet you an' all, but I'm afraid I'm gonna to have to blow you up."

You decide to mine the obvious joystick and also the part that you decided was the ignition key hole. Using the self-adhesive strips, you attach both mines to the control panel, placing them in those locations where you reckon they'll do the most damage.

You have no idea how powerful the explosives are, but assume they were used by the Moonbase Archaeologists for blasting Lunar rock during their excavations, so you guess they must be pretty potent. The blast will certainly destroy the control panel, probably the whole Pilot's Seat, and possibly demolish some of this chamber too.

Now turn to **133**.

166

You hit the 'Y' key. The screen replies immediately with a sombre automated message:

We are sorry to learn that a Moonbase Shackleton will be lost.

Please proceed by entering your Authorisation Codes.

You must now type both Authorisation Codes into the computer terminal. You need to do a calculation similar to that done at the Red Airlock earlier, and here's how:

Add all the individual digits of Lieutenant Lawson's code to give you Lawson's Total.

Now add all the individual digits of Commander King's code to give you King's Total.

Finally, you must add Lawson's Total to King's Total to give you your New Complete Total.*

The New Complete Total is the reference you should **now turn to.**

If you are unable to do this because, through stress or fear, you mistakenly believed you had both codes but actually don't, then please try to clear your thoughts, go back to **112** and rethink your situation.

For instance, if Lawson's code is 9979894078, then do the following sum: 9+9+7+9+8+9+4+0+7+8, which adds up to a Lawson's Total of 70. Then, if King's code is 99879, do the following sum: 9+9+8+7+9, which adds up to a King's Total of 42. Finally, add Lawson's Total to King's Total to give you your New Complete Total (in this case it would be; 70+42=112). So, the reference you would turn to in this example would be 112.

167

Standing on the Moons surface, you take a moment to gain your sense of balance in the slight gravity. The desolate and starkly-lit landscape is breathtaking, but also strangely ominous. The sound of your own irregular, gasping breaths, and the occasional gentle whir from within your suit, is all that can be heard. The intermittent and seemingly random whirs and clicks, you can only assume, is this futuristic spacesuit just doing its life-support thing. Your breathing, irregular pants and gasps, is down to an almost overwhelming sense of fear. You close your eyes and try a little stress-control exercise that Professor Wylie taught you.

"I am barefoot," you begin. "Standing on cool, dewy grass. In a fragrant meadow. On a balmy springtime morn."

You take a deep breath and slowly exhale. Now more in control of both your breathing and your fear, you open your eyes and survey the scene.

Now turn to **141.**

168

You step gingerly into the cage, and realise it's a three-sided affair with no closing door. Pressing yourself against the back of the cage, you grasp the first lever and tug it from neutral to the go position. You then mentally cross your fingers, grasp the second lever, and pull it full to its end stop.

"Goin' down."

The cage starts its descent, rapidly reaching an alarming speed as it plunges you into the stark and silent blackness of the depths of the mysterious Shackleton Well.

Now turn to **137**.

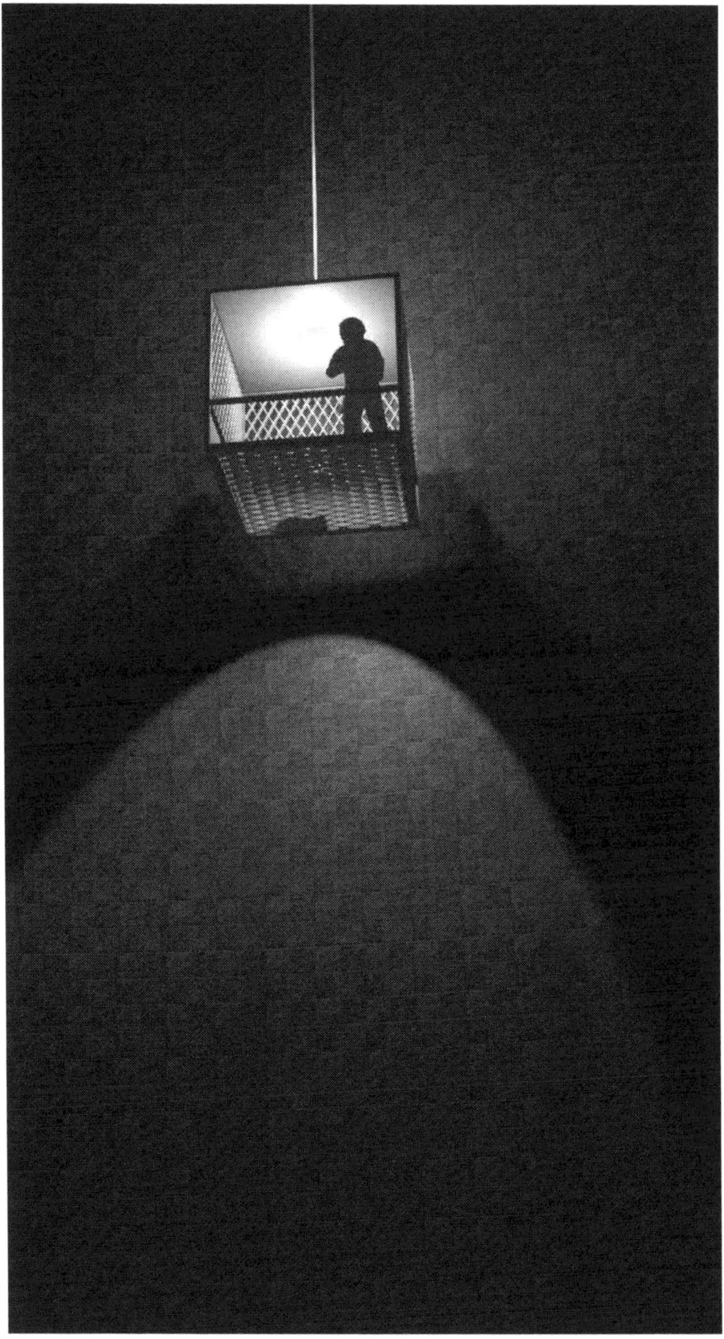

169

Also in the shelter are several bus-sized containers, like the type you've seen unloaded from ocean-going cargo ships. Clearly these containers have doors, and perhaps they're storage rooms, or workshops? You wonder if you have time to try breaking into one...

PLEASE BE AWARE: IN-SUIT AIR SUPPLY CURRENTLY AT 16%.

ESTIMATED TIME UNTIL REPLENISHMENT NECESSARY: 0.51 HOURS.

The sudden flash of projected text in front of your eyes startles you and, once read, leaves you further alarmed.

"Only half an hour left now?!" You blurt in reply. "But I've only been out here a few minutes!"

You realise that these spacesuits are supposed to be worn by trained professionals who don't nearly freak-out when they find themselves in outer-space situations, but your initial panicky gasping and frog-breathing has used up a lot of the suit's air reserve. Best you keep a level head from now on and continue to think of the cool, wet grass! Air, like time it seems, is in short supply right now.

You've got to keep moving.

Now turn to **119**.

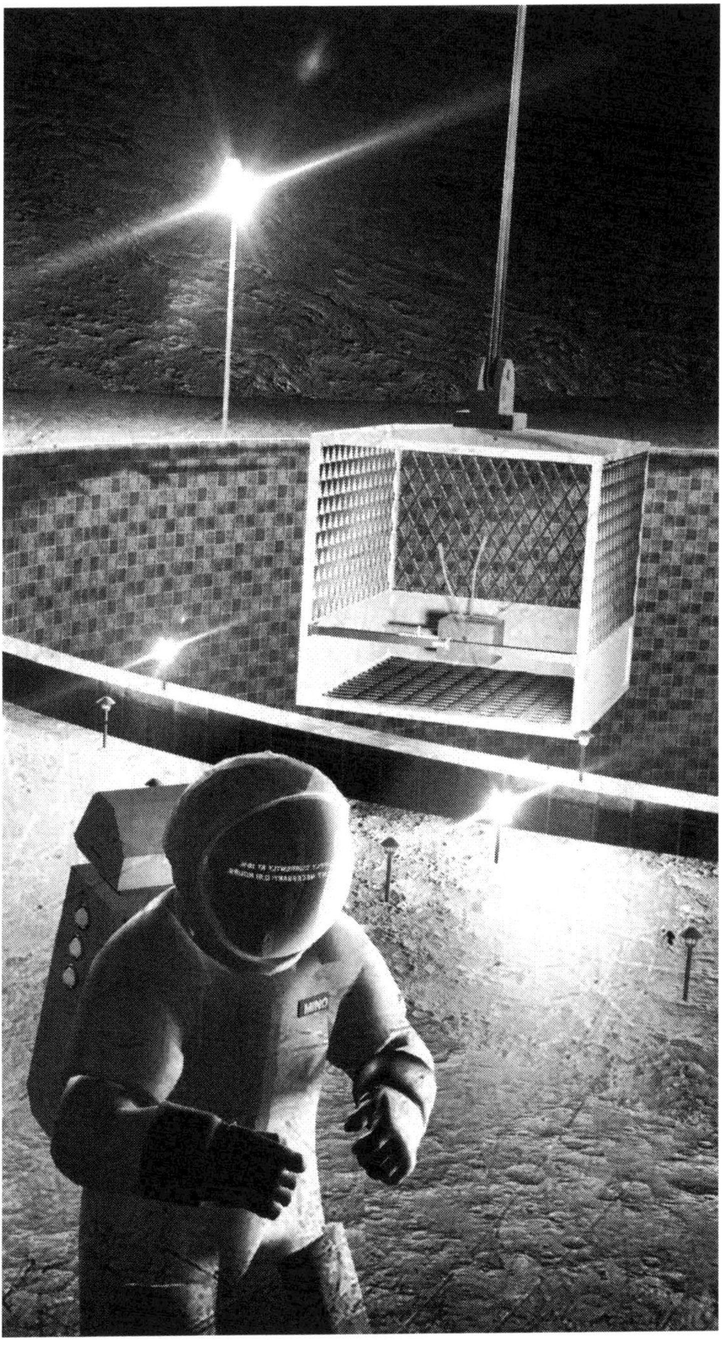

170

Suddenly, as if in response to your plea, that longed-for shimmering ball light reappears in the middle of the room, accompanied by the cacophonous crackle of raw, angry energy.

From cricket ball, through football, the light phases and pulses. Then it grows rapidly to a size that fills half the chamber as it morphs into the now-welcome sight of a horizontal tornado of swirling, spinning plasma and lightning. A familiar voice, as clear as a bell, issues from deep within the vaporous funnel...

"Hilary! I can see you," says Professor Wylie, with relief evident in her voice. "Can you see me?"

You peer into the heart of the Fugacious Spatial Vortex, having to squint against the harshness of the light, and there, in a giddying and weird sort of way, you see the Professor stood in the middle of her laboratory at SItU Headquarters. She seems to be about ten feet and a million miles away from you simultaneously.

"Professor! Get me out of here!" you yell.

"Run toward me, Hills, and quickly, I can't keep it open much longer. Be sure to duck, I want you to arrive home with your head!"

Without any hesitation you run towards the tunnel of blue light, ducking at the last moment...

For a few brief moments you're tumbling, weightlessly, intangibly, and seemingly downwards, through a tunnel of twisting blue-green light, and then...

...you fall into Professor Wylie's arms.

"Easy, Hills, I got you," you immediately hear her say, in her calm, reassuring tone.

For a moment you can still hear the crackle of raw, angry vortex energy, and then a loud bang as sparks and smoke fountain from out of the salvaged time-travel engine like a roman candle. You and the Professor watch together as the Fugacious Spatial Vortex flickers and fades.

Professor Wylie grabs a small fire extinguisher from her lab-bench and crosses to the crackling, flaring machinery. With just a few skillfully-directed blasts of CO_2 she brings the sparking and smouldering under control.

"Such a pity," she mutters sulkily. "Took me half-an-hour of frantic work to reassemble the Berwyn Device and get it operational. Probably beyond salvaging now."

The Professor, frowning and pouting like a petulant child, then turns her attention to you.

"Are you alright, Hilary?" Wylie's query is brusque.

"Yeah, I'll be okay," you reply. "Professor, I was on…"

"A Moonbase, one hundred years in the future, I gathered as much from the view the vortex gave me of the airlock, Hills," interrupts the Professor. "You know, you should never have put the battery in that Temporal Condenser Circuit you were working on. I'd just started to tweak the settings in the very heart of the Tachyon Capacitor, you see, so once you'd turned the Temporal Condenser on your fate was sealed."

You gape at the Professor, baffled by her explanation, and feeling hurt from her scalding. She sees the pain in your eyes and her expression immediately softens to one earnest concern as she slowly approaches and, with a somewhat awkward demeanour, takes your hands in hers.

"You're quite ashen and – goodness gracious me! – you're trembling," she says softly.

"What d'you expect? I fell through time! To the Moon!" You try to sound angry, but with all you've been through it sounds more like a mewle of disbelief.

"Y'know... ah... actually..." stumbles Professor Wylie. "It's probably my fault you ended up there; my carelessness that caused the localised Temporal-Spatial Distortion. I'm sorry, Hills."

"Saturmeks," you reply, and are unsure what else to add until you blurt. "They're going to destroy the Earth!"

"Saturmeks? Really? Look, Hilary, I'm a bit fuzzy on physical laws of time, but I do know that what you've just witnessed, no matter how immediate and raw it seems to you, hasn't happened yet. In fact, it won't happen for a hundred years... if it happens at all."

The Professor's voice trails off with a heavy sigh. You can see by the distant look in her eyes, and the way she nervously twiddles her necklace, that the thought of the terrifying experience you've undergone has just sunk in.

"Well, the Earth of here and now is under no imminent threat, that's the main thing," finishes the Professor disjointedly as she snaps out of her reverie. "Perhaps the return of the Saturmeks in the year 2074 is historical fact... er, future historical fact... that is to say, but it hasn't happened yet, and is a merely speculative future, but perhaps it will happen, and once it has happened, it will be fixed in history... er... If you get my meaning."

You can't help but to smile at Professor Wylie's fumbling exposition, and with the lifting of your spirits you realize that you're home and safe.

"Why don't you try to explain it to me again, over a nice big mug of sweet tea in the NAAFI," you suggest warmly.

"Hm, yes," the Professor grins. "I think a cup of tea and a slice of cake would..."

Professor Wylie pauses mid-sentence whilst looking you up and down quizzically.

"Just a minute... Is that a spacesuit you're wearing?!"

Now turn to the Epilogue at **200.**

171

Trembling through both fear and exhilaration, you hurry back down the main corridor to the Green Airlock. Passing into the Moonbase Living Quarters you firmly seal the doorway behind you, hoping that this section of Shackleton will be secure from the enormous explosion and subsequent decompression you're expecting any moment now.

You glance at your wristwatch; it's ten-forty. Half-an-hour, Professor Wylie promised from the other end of her Time Tornado, and nearly thirty minutes have now passed since you first found yourself on the Moon.

It's time to go!

Turn to **179**.

172

An odd and uncomfortable feeling of déjà vu settles upon you. You have the strangest feeling that you've done these very actions before, and are somehow reliving them. Although you don't yet fully realise it, you're caught in a time loop and doomed to experience the past two minutes over and over again with no chance of escape. Such is the fate of those who dare to dip randomly into events on this brutal Moon.

Now turn to **124**.

173

You decide that your only hope to await rescue.

"Please hurry, Professor," you mutter. "I really don't like the sound of being examined and interrogated."

Now turn to **052**.

174

During your brief exploration of the Moonbase so far, you discovered two explosive mining charges, which you feel you should now put to good use. Each mine, you noted at the time, had a serial number stamped onto it.

Please now add the first two digits of the first mine and the last two digits of the second mine together to result in a single figure. *

The number your arithmetic results in is the reference number you should **now turn to.**

If you are unable to do this because, through stress and fear, you mistakenly believed you possessed explosives but actually don't then please try to clear your thoughts, go back to **095** and rethink your situation.

For example, if you know that first mine's serial is 1234, and the second mine's serial is 5678, then you should do the following simple calculation: 12+78 which results in 90. So, in this example, you would now turn to 90.

175

"Hmm. Too risky," you whisper.

You gather up your set of assorted screwdrivers, wrenches and pliers, and slide the tri-fold wallet back into your pocket. You take one last look about the Storeroom and, seeing nothing else of immediate use or interest, you exit via the steel door.

Now turn to **082**.

176

You're really not the kind of person who'd spend thirty minutes sat on your hands and doing nothing while Saturmeks are plotting Earth's doom! You decide that you have more than time enough to explore the Moonbase a little and gather some intel, so turn your attention back to the airlock door.

The Airlock door is a large, circular affair with a complicated-looking locking mechanism located just below its portal window. Stencilled onto the door are clearly-written instructions and pictograms of how to operate it, and so you follow the simple three-step guide. You turn the green dial on the left of the door from 'X' to 'O', then press the green stud-button on the right of the door when it lights up, and finally pull the red handle, located on the central lock itself, downwards.

The door swings slowly outward, driven by entirely silent motors, and you step cautiously out into the corridor.

The lengthy corridor which stretches out ahead of you is featureless and purely utilitarian; no decor or personal touches give you any insight into the kind of people who occupied this sterile place. It's also quite wide, and you could probably drive a lorry down it and barely brush the sides or ceiling.

You see that the corridor terminates with another sturdy Airlock door about fifty yards ahead of you. Halfway down the corridor is a crossroads junction with smaller secondary corridors leading off to the left and right.

You're in very dangerous territory! You know that the occupants of Shackleton have been slaughtered by the Saturmek invaders, and you could be next if you put a foot wrong! Hardly daring to breathe, you creep slowly and quietly up the length of the passage.

Your cautious and circumspect pace brings you to the junction where a narrower East-West passage transects this main corridor. The Moonbase remains eerily silent as you pause, look about yourself, and consider your options.

Now turn to **072**.

177

A swift, furtive walk sees you back at the intersection. You glance around, wondering what's best to do next.

From where you now stand, you can see that the North Corridor ends after about twenty-five yards with the white, double doors marked *Operations Centre*; the source of an ominous electronic heart-beat sound.

The West Passageway, which leads off to your left, is quite short and ends at a steel-grey coloured single door simply marked as *Stores*.

If you were to head south, via the Green Airlock, you would find yourself heading back the way you originally came, and could very quickly return to the Orange Airlock where you first fell into this nightmare. Professor Wylie did tell you not to move from there, after all.

Should you now:

Head North up the corridor to investigate the Operations Centre? If this is your choice, turn to **089**.

Take the passageway to your left and see if the Storeroom might offer up something? To do this, turn to **028**.

Or should you get yourself out of harm's way by returning to the South end of the Moonbase, and back to the relative safety of the Orange Airlock? There you can await rescue by the Professor. If this is your choice, turn to **031**.

178

You need to do some arithmetic, just to satisfy Lawson that you're on the level; add up the individual digits of King's Authorisation Code to give you a single number, then multiply that number by two. The resulting number is the reference you should **now turn to.** *

If you were just bluffing to comfort the dying Lieutenant, now's the time to admit you told her a white lie, and turn to **014**.

For example, if you know the Commander's Code is 123, then do the following calculation: 1+2+3 which results in 6. Now multiply the result by 2, giving you 12. So, the reference you turn to in this instance would therefore be 12.

179

You hurriedly open the Orange Airlock door, and as you step into the chamber the entire Moonbase is rocked by a massive, reverberating explosion. You regain your footing and slam the door shut, locking and sealing it.

The Moonbase is rocked again by an even greater seismic blast; the mines you set must have triggered a secondary and more powerful explosion in the Operations Centre! Daring to peer through the porthole window you are unnerved to see that the corridor outside begins to buckle and warp. In the distance, the Green Airlock is blasted open by an energy beam and a severely dented and scorched Saturmek Drone struggles laboriously on its stuttering, buckled motivator-ball to flee ground zero. You continue to watch with a mixture of horror and fascination as the Green Airlock, a portion of the corridor, and then the hapless Saturmek survivor are consumed by an undulating and expanding ruddy-orange ball of unearthly fire! The seething, gaseous inferno billows down the corridor towards your refuge with all the determined and unstoppable pace of freshly-spewed lava, gorging itself on the very structure of the Moonbase as it approaches.

The ancient artefact, you realise, must have housed a considerable reserve of long-dormant energy which you've now released... and it's heading your way!

Now turn to **181.**

180

"Operations Centre, eh?" you muse as you produce your ever-faithful set of assorted scientific tools from your back pocket. "I reckon that's where I need to head as soon as I've popped this open."

Knelt before the Airlock door, with your set of assorted screwdrivers, wrenches and pliers laid-out neatly on the floor in front of you, you examine a conspicuous access panel below the circuit-breaker style switch, and carefully consider how to proceed. You're pleased to see that even in whatever future year this is, when man lives on the Moon, they still use good old-fashioned counter-sunk flathead screws to fix stuff to things! The panel is off in moments using your dinky screwdriver.

You're surprised to see how basic the mechanism behind the panel is, but then this door has a lock as a safety measure – to prevent accidental opening at inappropriate times – it's not a security door designed to keep heisters from the Crown Jewels or anything. There's a complicated circuit-board which looks to be the bit that controls the movement of the mechanism, but it's all blackened and melted. That's what the Saturmek meant when it said it had secured the door from the outside; it had given it a quick blast of its gun to melt the electronics and make it inoperable. There's no damage, though, to the actual steel mechanical workings.

"This should be a piece of cake," you chirp. "Manual override, Hilary Hills-style, coming up!"

Using a miniature hand-drill from a vintage Mecanno set, you gouge a decently deep hole into the central locking gear, near the edge of its circumference, and then you jam in your screwdriver as a make-shift crank handle. With a few determined rotations of the locking gear, which offers only a little resistance against the Saturmek-inflicted heat-damage, the door makes a satisfying clunk as the locking bolts slip from their housings. The Airlock Door swings silently open as you gather up your tools and rise to your feet with the air of a job well done.

Add 10 points to your Savvy Score and turn to **184.**

181

You've destroyed the Saturmeks, and Earth is safe, but you realise your heroic act has potentially come with such cost to yourself!

Trembling, you turn your back on the fearsome sight of the encroaching fireball, and crouch into a foetal position.

"Professor," you cry out. "Where are you?!"

Then you add quietly, "I'm not ready to die!"

Now turn to **052.**

182

You slowly raise you hands in surrender as the Saturmek approaches.

Now turn to **008.**

183

You're definitely in two minds about things. The extreme danger of the situation you find yourself in doesn't escape your attention, so perhaps staying in this Airlock awaiting your imminent extraction from peril – as promised by Professor Wylie – would be the safest, not to mention the most sensible, course of action. But Earth is in even greater danger than you, and to sit on your bum doing nothing while the Saturmeks are just down the corridor plotting its utter annihilation seems pretty lame.

You study the Airlock Door, which only moments ago the Saturmek Drone had boasted was sealed, secured and unopenable from your side, and you imagine what the locking mechanism inside must look like. It's all part-and-parcel of your scientific method; using your imagination, like X-ray vision, to picture the lay-out of the gears, cogs an' stuff within the lock. You have, in your back pocket, neatly and lovingly arranged in a battered tri-fold wallet, your ever-reliable scientific toolkit, and you wonder if you should have a go at opening that Airlock.

Of course, your captor might have booby-trapped or alarmed the door against tampering – it would be in keeping with a devious Saturmek to do that – and if you were to be caught trying to escape you very much doubt the Saturmeks would be as lenient as they were last time you inconvenienced them. In fact, you're pretty sure the Red Chief would most likely forget any curiosity it has about the whys-and-wherefores of how you come to be on the Moonbase and just kill you on the spot.

Yeah, Hills, choices, choices...

Will you have a go at pickin' an' trickin' the lock on the Airlock Door, with the intention of escaping your prison and meddling further in the Saturmeks schemes? If you want to try this, turn to **180**.

If, however, you think that the Saturmeks have probably pre-empted any escape attempt you might make, and you're likely to get yourself killed by causing them any further bother, then you might want to take a seat and wait for Professor Wylie to re-establish contact... perhaps she can sort this mess out. If you think that this is the most sensible course of action, then turn to **173**.

184

Summoning up every ounce of your courage, feeling a steely determination to save your own planet from the abominable and genocidal Saturmeks at any cost, you silently and swiftly exit the South Airlock.

"Right," you announce to no one in particular. "Let's see what mischief I can cause in and around the Operations Centre!"

Keeping a crouched posture and staying close to the wall, you scurry the short distance Northwards up the main corridor towards the Green Airlock.

Now turn to **030**.

185

Lawson's steely gaze meets yours as she manages to flash you a smile of encouragement.

"I've got a cyber-chip in my head," she continues between laboured gasps of pain. "Hacked into the Saturmek comms. Four of 'em on the base; a red leader, a scientist, and two thugs. They're all in the Operations Centre at the top of the North Corridor now. They think they've killed everyone, so their guard's down. Didn't reckon on us, eh?"

You brave a sympathetic smile as Lawson's dying stare meets your eyes.

"Go back to the junction and head up through the Green North Airlock. Take the right passageway off the Main Corridor to the Red Airlock and the Decontamination Chamber. That chamber leads to the excavation site... and the Sterilisation Protocol Alpha One Self-Destruct Console. Enter Rex's code... enter my code... then set the countdown to blow this place and the Saturmeks to hell."

Lawson exhales a long, mechanically-assisted sigh as her head lolls limply to one side, then the dorm falls silent.

Lawson's dead.

And Earth dies in just a few hours.

It's time to go!

Will you attempt to save the Earth by undertaking a dangerous mission to blow-up the base? If you want to take this chance then add 10 points to your Savvy Score and turn to **041.**

Or should you put all your faith in being rescued by Professor Wylie before time runs out, and hope she has a solution to this terrible peril the Earth is in? If this is the better option then add 10 points to your Savvy Score and turn to **013.**

186

A short sneak up the corridor sees you arrive at the double-doors. You find that they're actually constructed of the same plastic-like material as the rest of the base, but have been quite cleverly painted with a faux-wood finish by an artistic hand. It certainly lends the communal dining area a cosy and homely feel for any homesick spacemen.

Peering through the large windows tells you nothing; the room beyond is entirely in darkness, and all is deathly silent.

You gently push on the doors and they swing effortlessly open. Gathering your courage, and with a furtive glance behind you to ensure you are not being observed, you step into the Moonbase Shackleton canteen.

Now turn to **032.**

187

Professor Wylie looks down to her bowl, picks up the spoon again and prods idly at the cooling suet.

"You know the Saturmeks by reputation, Hills," she says softly. "They're ruthless murderers, and you showed great courage going up against a squad of them alone."

"You did tell me to stay put," you add. "But I had to try something, sorry."

"I did tell you to stay put, yes," replies the Professor, slowly looking up from her pudding to meet your eyes with a mischievous smile. "But... Earth threatened with utter destruction, a squad of Saturmeks running amok, the Moonbase crew massacred; and at great personal risk you took it upon yourself to save the World. That's my Hilary Hills!"

"It's good to be home safe, Professor," you smile.

"Relieved to have you home safe, Hills," returns the Professor with a broad beam. "And it's also fascinating to learn that the Saturmeks are still at large out there in space. We had hoped the germ bombs devised back in '97 had finished them off for good, but always suspected that there might be a few survivors that escaped. It's a pity that current rocket technology doesn't allow us to take the fight to them, but at least it seems we have decades to prepare."

"I'm pretty certain there were no Saturmek survivors this time," you say.

"Not much chance of that, from what you've told me," Professor Wylie affirms. "There must've been a massive energy source dammed-up in that strange stone key. The Saturmeks intended to use it as a means to destroy Earth, but ended up being destroyed by it. Hoist with their own petard! Well done, Hills. I'm very proud of you."

"Professor Wylie..." interrupts a familiar voice. You both look over to see Captain Knight hurrying to your table.

"Top of the morning to you, Andrew," hails the Professor. "Well, what demands is Sir Clive about to make on my precious time now?"

"He asks that you join him at Number 10 Downing Street immediately," replies Knight.

"Oh, yes? Hobnobbing with the PM, is he?"

"Not exactly," explains Captain Knight. "Apparently, during a Cabinet Meeting this morning, the Prime Minister began smoking..."

"So, Mr. Wilson enjoys to puff on a pipe," interrupts Professor Wylie somewhat testily. "Filthy habit, but is this really a matter for SItU?"

"No, not that kind of smoking, Professor," explains Knight patiently. "He started to smoke and then burst into flames. Turns out he was a robot."

"Goodness gracious, I wonder what happened to the real PM?!" exclaims the Professor as she rises from the table. "Kidnapped and substituted, no doubt. But by whom? Coming, Hills?"

You jump to your feet, raring to go.

"This has all the hallmarks of a sinister foreign plot against Britain, Hills," calls back the Professor as she breezes out of the room.

"Never a dull moment," you quip to Captain Knight, and then you chase after Professor Wylie on your way to a new adventure.

The End.

188

Knelt before the cabinet, with your set of screwdrivers, wrenches and pliers laid out on the floor in front of you, you examine the Blasting Ordnance cabinet's lock, confident that this will be quite an easy pick for you. However, peering into the keyhole with your purloined penlight torch, and also studying where the cabinet door's edges meet its frame, you glimpse what might be some electrical wiring within the cabinet, which seems to lead to where the bolt-action would slide.

"An alarm system, a booby trap, or something less sinister?" you muse.

Now turn to **060**.

189

"Have you seen Commander King anywhere?" Lawson asks hopefully. "Do you know his Authorisation Code?"

If you know Commander Rex King's Authorisation Code then turn to **178**.

If you don't know the code Lawson is asking about, then you must turn to **014**.

190

Lu, the operator you spoke to at Lovelock Beacon, calls an Earth Defence Red Alert immediately after receiving your Mayday. Good work, Hilary.

Now turn to **055**.

191

Your conscience can't allow you to leave that poor man out there if there's a chance that he's still alive and, given the urgency of the situation, you think that running up and down corridors looking for someone to help would just waste vital minutes. You take a look at the Spacesuits, neatly arranged on their hooks, they all look identical; the same generic size, shape and cut. You've never worn a Spacesuit before, but have seen several in use during your recent months at SItU, so how difficult could putting one on be? You take one down from its hook to discover it was obscuring an instructional notice on the wall entitled:

The Windak Emergency Evacuation Pressure Suit.

Instructions for Use.

You glance over the tutorial, paying closer attention to the diagrams than the text, and get the gist of it. The suit is designed to be slipped on in just moments; it seals and adjusts itself to the wearer's figure, and the helmet self-locks to the neck seal. The suit is designed for emergency use only; should the Moonbase need to be evacuated, and if any crew find themselves unable to get to their own Spacesuits, they can survive outside wearing one of these... for a while. You note that battery life and air supply limited to three hours.

"So, in a nutshell, this is a space-age life jacket," you summarise to yourself as you clamber into your chosen suit and zip it up from crotch-to-chin.

The helmet, which you grab from beneath the bench, is of a classic goldfish bowl design. As you slip it over your head, the neck-seal of your suit reaches up to meet it with an unnerving suction sound. Then, with a satisfying gulp-clunk, the transparent globe is firmly secured. A burst of short whirs and clicks issue from the suit as life support systems activate.

You head to the Airlock Door and look for a means of opening it. Being an Emergency Exit, the operating procedure is simple; a chunky handle in the middle of the door is set on lock, an arrow indicates you turn the handle to depressurise and unlock it. Without hesitation you grasp the handle and give it a hearty twist. From an unseen speaker somewhere in the room a pre-recorded female voice announces, in calming tones, that emergency decompression has commenced. You feel a gust of air tug at the fabric of your suit as the voice begins to count down the seconds from fifteen, and then the suit inflates and stiffens about your body in response to the venting atmosphere. The room falls profoundly silent before the recorded countdown reaches three.

"Two... one..." you count to yourself.

The Orange Airlock Door swings noiselessly outward, causing a small eddy of surface dust to rise and curl like smoke.

"One-sixth gravity from now on," you remind yourself as you warily step over the threshold and plant your foot in the Lunar soil. "Tread carefully!"

Add 10 points to your Savvy Score.

Now turn to **071.**

192

The following thirty minutes drag by, and then you spy Professor Wylie return to the NAAFI accompanied by Sergeant Cox. The Professor remains at the doorway, and you notice with dismay that she looks uncharacteristically aloof and officious with her arms folded, as she observes matters from afar. The Sergeant hurriedly approaches the table where you still sit alone nursing an empty tea mug. You've had half an hour to mull over what the Professor said – and *how* she said it – and you suspect you know what happens next.

"Hilary Hills..." begins Sergeant Cox.

"Morning, Mark," you interrupt. "Is it time?"

"Yes, Hills," replies Cox sharply. "You are to accompany me and Professor Wylie to a meeting with Sir Clive in his office."

"Come on, then," you say as you rise from the table. "Let's get it over with. I'm imagine this won't take long."

The march through SItU's labyrinth of underground corridors is quite a brief one, but every step of the way is made awkward by Professor Wylie's stern, and perhaps introspective, silence. Before very long you arrive at a sturdy wooden door which Sergeant Cox raps upon with his chunky, ruddy knuckles and, without waiting for a response, opens. The sergeant gestures that you should enter with a terse sideways jerk of his head.

Now turn to **113**.

193

There's a slight tremble to your hands, a touch of nerves no doubt, as you're taking quite a risk. But the lock offers you little trouble as you pick at and jiggle the barrel with your kit, and it's the work of less than a minute before you hear the satisfying click of the lock surrendering. Very carefully you open the cabinet door just a fraction and slip your fingers into the crack to feel around the frame for those suspicious wires you spotted. You satisfy yourself that they run up the inside of the cabinet from bottom to top but do not appear to connect with the lock in any obvious way. You take a deep breath and hold it, cross your fingers, and fully open the cabinet door...

Now turn to **093**.

194

You find walking in one-sixth Earth gravity, in a *proper* pressurised spacesuit, isn't as easy as Fairfax and Cardew made it look on telly.[*] And they didn't have the advantage of 21st Century technology, you note, hearing the clicking and whirring of little servomotors within your garment which seem to compensate for every potential misstep and clumsy lurch you almost make.

"Walking in these clunky boots isn't helping," you mutter to yourself. "More of a sandals person, me."

Now turn to **102**.

[*] This, of course, refers to Flight Lieutenant Deirdre Fairfax and Wing Commander Percival Cardew, the first people to walk on the Moon, 3rd June 1969. See the Acknowledgement section at the rear of this book for more information.

195

The return elevator ride to the Lunar surface seems to take an eternity, and with each passing minute, within your increasingly claustrophobic spacesuit, it's getting a little harder to catch your breath. Looking aloft, you're relieved to see the nearing of the lights on the Moon's surface.

**ALERT: IN-SUIT AIR SUPPLY CURRENTLY AT 3%.
REPLENISHMENT ESSENTIAL IN: 0.05 HOURS.**

"That's taken a whole five minutes…" you think, but waste no breath voicing your dismay. The crane slows and then stops the paying-in of the cable as the cage draws to a halt level with the lip of the Shackleton Well, and you fix your determined gaze on the Grey Airlock Door some distance across the Lunar surface.

Now turn to **134.**

196

"What have you to report?" you hear the Red Saturmek demand of its subordinate.

"Resistance has been easily neutralised," replies the Green Drone. "As we expected, the Moonbase is currently staffed by only eight humans. The seven present have been slain."

"Another lies dead outside," adds the Red Saturmek. "We now hold the Moonbase! We can immediately commence phase two of the Saturmek destruction of Earth!"

From behind the door, you stifle a gasp and sink down a little further.

Add 10 points to your Savvy Score and turn to **076.**

197

You continue to listen as the out-of-focus video descends into a disturbing series of shallow, gasping pants and bloody splutters, until finally and mercifully the recording falls silent. You switch off the late Commander Rex King's Incident Log, shaken by what you're seen and heard. You know about Saturmeks, of course; everyone does. It's almost unthinkable that they're on the Moon right now – whenever *right now* is – but you have to believe your own eyes and ears. The dreaded Saturmeks are back, and they've murdered the Moonbase Commander. Uncertain of what to do next, you whisper an almost inaudible plea for Professor Wylie to come and rescue you.

Add 10 points to your Savvy Score and turn to **048**.

198

Instead of forging ahead into the Operations Area of Moonbase Shackleton, you retrace your steps back to the junction. Pausing here for just a moment, you consider what to do next.

If you haven't already, you might choose to take the West Passage to investigate the Canteen and Kitchen. If you think this is a worthwhile venture, turn to **186.**

Alternatively, you might prefer to head down the East Corridor to see if the Dormitory is occupied. To do this, turn to **067.**

If you've already explored both these areas, then you should once again head North up the passage to the Green Airlock and, without further hesitation, open it. To see what lies ahead, turn to **074.**

199

Although you fear the Saturmeks, you fear being blown to pieces more, and so you sprint up the East Corridor with reckless abandon. Your borrowed spacesuit now hangs baggily about your wiry frame, but it doesn't impede your frantic gait as you take a sharp left at the junction and barrel down the Central Corridor towards the Green Airlock.

It's high time Professor Wylie was making a reconnection, so you're through the Green Door in moments and darting towards the Orange South Airlock where you originally tumbled arse-backwards into this nightmare.

Now turn to **118**.

200 - Epilogue

You take a long, satisfying sip from your mug of strong, sweet NAAFI tea, washing down your elevenses of hot-buttered toast and marmalade. Professor Wylie is tucking into her second helping of jam roly-poly and custard with great gusto.

"This really is quite excellent," she remarks between over-loaded spoonsful. "Mrs. Mallard has surpassed herself this morning; I really must thank her before we get back to work."

The Professor's earnest enthusiasm for some of life's little indulgences makes you smile as you quietly reflect on everything you've just told her. Professor Wylie had listened intently, without comment or interruption, and with care and concern softening her aquiline features, but there was also a fierce curiosity burning in her eyes. And now she's talking about her pudding as if what you've just been through is no big deal!

"You know, Hills, I am sorry about what happened," Wylie then utters with a sigh.

You realise that the Professor was just filling the silence while she mulled over the crazy story you babbled to her. Now that she's had a few moments to consider what she's learnt, the Professor puts down her spoon and is ready for a discussion.

"I realise how very disconcerting – alarming, even – this whole experience must've been for you," Professor Wylie continues. "But you have provided us, at least, with a fascinating glimpse of possible future events."

"You can say that again," you reply. "Finding myself on the Moon was one heck of a freaky trip to say the least, but I did my best to keep my head straight, and I hope I was savvy enough to do the right thing while I was up there."

What are Professor Vyvian Wylie's thoughts on how you conducted yourself during your solo adventure? It's time to find out. Please total-up your Savvy Score, and then read the directions below carefully.

If your Savvy Score is less than 50, then turn to **085**.

If your Savvy Score is 50 or more and ends with a zero, then turn to **044**.

If your Savvy Score is 50 or more and ends with a five, then turn to **187**.

If your Savvy Score is 50 or more and ends with a seven, then turn to **069**.

If your Savvy Score is 50 or more and ends with a nine, then turn to **027**.

A derelict Saturmek casing, from the failed invasion of 1897, on display today in the British Museum, London. The relic, discovered during dredging of the Thames near Waterloo Bridge in 1952, and was reconstructed and restored by Thames Waterway Volunteers before donation to the museum.

Acknowledgements

Throughout this science fiction novel references are made to brands and products which are wholly and entirely the intellectual and legal property of noted and respected companies, organisations and/or persons. The authors of *Brutal Moon* wish to acknowledge these particulars of ownership below.

References to *Prof. Q.* and *Bernie* in this work allude to Nigel Kneale's fictional scientist, Professor Bernard Quatermass, a character originally created by Kneale for BBC Television.

Mott The Hoople were a five-piece British rock band in the 1970s, best known for their hits *All the Young Dudes* and *Roll Away the Stone*.

Eveready is a trademark ™ of Eveready Battery Company, Inc., owned by Energizer Holdings.

Silk Cut is a British brand of cigarettes, currently owned and manufactured by Gallaher Group, a division of Japan Tobacco.

Spirit in the Sky is a song written and originally recorded by Norman Greenbaum, and produced by Erik Jacobson. It was first released in 1969. All rights owned by Erik Jacobson.

The Joker is a song written by Eddie Curtis, Ahmet Ertegun, and Steve Miller, and produced by Steve Millar. It was first released in 1973. © 1973 Sailor Records.

I'm the Urban Spaceman is a song written by Neil Innes, and originally recorded by the Bonzo Dog Doo-Dah Band in 1968. It was produced by Paul McCartney and Gus Dudgeon working under the pseudonym of *Apollo C. Vermouth*. © Parlophone Records Ltd, a Warner Music Group Company.

Brodie's Notes are succinct study guides for students of English Literature written by experts in the field, and published by Palgrave Macmillan.

Windak was a trade name used by the Macclesfield-based company Baxter Woodhouse Taylor, and had been in use since the Second World War on items of heated flying clothing and a series of full pressure suits known as Windak Suits. Although Baxter Woodhouse Taylor ceased operations in February 2005, in *Time & Fate*'s fictional universe the company were contracted to work for the *Britannic Experimental Rocket Group* in the 1950s, and enjoyed great success fabricating garments for off-World work and travel well into the 2100s.

Erich von Däniken is a Swiss author of several books which hypothesise that extraterrestrials influenced early human culture. His work includes the 1968-published best-seller, *Chariots of the Gods?*.

The Michelin Man, also known as Bibendum, is the official mascot of the Michelin Tyre Company and is a trademark ™ of Compagnie Générale des Établissements Michelin SCA.

Perspex is a registered trademark ™ of Perspex International, considered by many to be the world's leading manufacturer of acrylic sheet and composite products. The trademarked name is particularly synonymous with transparent plastic products of quality.

Meccano is a metal model construction system created in 1898 by Frank Hornby in Liverpool, United Kingdom. Mecanno is a trademark™ of Spin Master Ltd, Canada.

Land Rover is a British brand of predominantly four-wheel drive, off-road capable vehicles. Land Rover is a trademark™ of Jaguar Land Rover Limited.

The character of Sweep™, the grey glove puppet dog with long black ears who has appeared in all permutations of *The Sooty Show*™ since 1957, is property of Cadells Ltd / Entertainment Ltd. In *Time & Fate*'s fictional universe Sweep™ was also, ironically, the lucky mascot of one of Moonbase Shackleton's crewmembers.

Sinclair Research Ltd is a British consumer electronics company founded by Clive Sinclair in Cambridge in 1973. The Sinclair Scientific calculator was a 12-function, pocket-sized device introduced in 1974, dramatically undercutting in price of other calculators available at the time. In *Time & Fate*'s fictional universe, it was Sir Clive Sinclair himself that gifted a number of his company's calculators to his good friend, Vyvian Wylie, for beta testing.

The first people to walk on the Moon, on July 21, 1969, were the celebrated American Astronauts, Commander Neil Armstrong and Colonel Buzz Aldrin, whilst Major General Michael Collins remained in the Command Module. However, in *Time & Fate's* fictional timeline, it was Great Britain, an unannounced contender, that took the World entirely by surprise by winning the Space Race with their Top-Secret *Bulldog 3* Mission. The Lunar Lander, *Churchill*, touched-down on the Moon's Surface on the 3rd June 1969. Manning the *Churchill* were Wing Commander Percival Cardew and Flight Lieutenant Deirdre Fairfax, whilst Group Captain Sir Douglas Bader remained overseeing events from the Command Module. The British Government had instructed that Cardew would lead the exit of the *Churchill*, thus making the first man to walk on the Moon an Englishman. Percy Cardew, however, being a consummate gentleman, was heard over the airwaves to politely say at the critical moment; "*Ladies first, naturally*" and so the historic first steps on the Lunar surface were taken by Deirdre Fairfax.

BRUTAL MOON

A Time & Fate Adventure Gamebook

Created and Written by
Andrew Morris and Laura Dodd

Editor
Laura Dodd

Design and Illustrations
Andrew Morris

Mercy Buckets
Mino Atasiei
Lu Lovelock
Ted & Jean Morris
Chloe Mortimer
Erwin S. Ramrod

Website
News on forthcoming publications, and exclusive *Brutal Moon* merchandise can be found at **timeandfate.com**

Contact
The authors can be contacted via the website above.

And Finally...
If you've enjoyed *Brutal Moon*, please consider leaving a spoiler-free positive review on Amazon™, or your favourite social media platforms. Thank you.

Wylie and Hills will return.

Hilary Hills

Carrying -

Small pocket wallet containing scientific tools; screwdriver, hand drill, pliers and stuff like that.

How Savvy am I? -

Plenty of room overleaf to <u>make a note of</u> things →

Notes

Notes

```
THANK YOU FOR VISITING
MOONBASE SHACKLETON.
   WE HOPE YOU ENJOYED
           YOUR STAY.
```

Printed in Great Britain
by Amazon